JUST A FUN LITTLE SKIRT...

Mr. Hot opened my door for me and held out his hand. "Your chariot awaits."

Total hunk. I put my hand in his and let him assist me into the truck. After all, my fun little skirt didn't work too well for climbing into pickup trucks.

Rand smiled at me. "You look cute."

I grinned. "Thanks."

"She looks like she's going to a party, not camping," Tad said.

My good feeling immediately faded and I threw a glare back at him. "Why can't you be nice?"

"I just said you looked like you were going to a party. I wasn't disagreeing that you looked cute."

"So you think I look cute?"

Tad opened his mouth to respond, then looked at Rand. He shut his mouth and leaned back in the seat. What had Tad been about to say? Would he have admitted he thought I was cute? Or would it have been some other insult?

And why did I care anyway?

WHO NEEDS BOYS?

STEPHIE DAVIS

SMOOCH **NEW YORK CITY**

To JR, for believing in me more than I believe in myself.

Thanks to my fantastic agent Michelle Grajkowski for her unending support, and to my wonderful editor Kate Seaver and the rest of the Dorchester Publishing team for all their hard work on my behalf. Without all of you, none of my dreams would have come true.

SMOOCH ®

May 2005

Published by

Dorchester Publishing Co., Inc.
200 Madison Avenue
New York, NY 10016

ISBN 0-8439-5397-7

The name "SMOOCH" and its logo are trademarks of Dorchester Publishing Co., Inc.

Printed in the United States of America.

Visit us on the web at www.smoochya.com.

WHO NEEDS BOYS?

Chapter One

I was heavily immersed in my fantasy about beautiful beaches, endless ocean and oodles of tanned, hot men when my friend Frances elbowed me with a shot of ugly reality.

Latin class.

Ugh.

I pulled out a piece of paper and a pen and jotted her a note. "Why'd you do that? I was fantasizing about Los Angeles. Less than a month away."

She wrote back, "Listen to Mr. Novak."

Well, that sure was fun. Frances and I didn't have the same attitude toward school, homework and teachers. She studied. I didn't. She listened to teachers. I daydreamed. Why should I take school seriously? It wasn't as if it would make a difference, and who cared what I did anyway? No one. So I did what I wanted.

"Allie? Are you with us?"

I smiled at my teacher. Yeah, sure, he was cute for an old guy, but he was still my teacher. "Of course."

"Good." He turned back to the board and finished writing an e-mail address. "During the summer, I run a farm stand. I grow most of my own produce in the fields behind the stand. I need kids to work for me this summer. If any of you are interested, e-mail me."

I raised my hand. "Are we the only people you're asking?" This sounded like a social opportunity if there were boys present. "Or will there be boys there?" Might as well lay it out there. It wasn't as if everyone didn't already know why I was asking.

Mr. Novak folded his arms across his chest and gave me the Look. You know, the one where the teacher is wondering what in the world he's going to do with you. I get it a lot. "Actually, there will be quite a few boys working there as well."

A titter zipped through the room. I go to an all-girls school in Massachusetts, just outside Boston, and it's hard to meet boys unless you take initiative. Like me. I initiate a lot and I have plenty of boys in my life.

I'm not about to sit around waiting for them to track me down, because they won't. It's a fact of life. It's not that I'm particularly ugly or anything; it's just that boys don't approach girls, at least not with the frequency I want.

So I take charge.

That's what I'm all about. Taking charge. Being independent. It's not like I want to be like that, but I have no choice. My life would suck if I let it.

"Although there will be boys present, this is not a social event." Mr. Novak appeared to be addressing the class, but he was looking right at me. "It's hard work and I expect full commitment. Anything less and I'll have to let you go. I have a business to run and I need dedicated employees." He nodded to the class. "That's it. Let me know."

Yeesh. He needed to chill. It wasn't as if I was going to actually sign up and ruin his business. I had bigger plans for this summer.

"You want to do it?" Frances asked.

I packed up my notebook. "I can't. I'm going to L.A. for the summer to visit my dad, remember?" I was so psyched. I hadn't been to see him much since he'd divorced my mom six years ago, but he was engaged to some woman now and he wanted me to get to know her. Los Angeles in the summer. How cool would that be? Wonder what movie stars I'd see? Maybe I'd get discovered and become a famous actress and never have to come back.

Frances frowned. "For the whole summer? I thought it was only a couple weeks."

I fell into step with her. "The whole summer. Isn't that cool? I'm going to spend three glorious months at the beach."

She lifted her brow. "Sounds productive."

I rolled my eyes. "Lighten up, Frances. You're productive enough for both of us." And she was. Frances was on full scholarship at our school, and she got straight As. Her parents were determined that Frances would be the first member of the family to go to college. She took that responsibility seriously. Too seriously. Which meant it was up to me to have enough fun for both of us, since she was certainly doing two people's worth of work.

"I'm going to do it," Frances announced.

"Why? You already have a boyfriend. You don't need to meet boys." I still couldn't believe studious Frances and bad boy Theo were dating. She kept him out of trouble, and he got her to loosen up a little. Not a lot, but a little. They'd never last when he went to college in the fall, but that was okay. Then I'd have her back and I wouldn't have to share her anymore.

"I need the money."

"Oh." Stupid, Allie. I should have realized that.

Money was always short at her house. "Then it's a good idea. You should do it."

She nodded. "I wonder if Natalie and Blue want to work there too."

Natalie and Blue? So the three of them could have some majorly fun adventure this summer at the farm stand without me? I'd come back in September and they'd have all sorts of private jokes that I wouldn't be a part of? "Um . . . I doubt they'll want to do it. Blue will be hanging out with Colin and Natalie probably has running camp or something."

Frances shot me a look. "What's your problem?"

"I don't have a problem. What's yours?"

"You. You're my problem. Why are you being weird? Natalie and Blue will totally go for it and we'll have fun. Maybe we'll even get Natalie a boyfriend so she can double with me and Blue."

While I'm out in L.A. with my dad and his new woman. Alone. Missing out.

I lifted my chin. No, this was fine. I was going to have a great summer. So there. It wouldn't matter that I'd miss out on their fun. I'd create my own and it would be way better.

Besides, I'd be with my dad. Nothing could top that.

* * *

We met Natalie and Blue at three o'clock at the town common. It was a huge grassy area flanked by some trees. On sunny, warm days, it was always pretty crowded with people enjoying the weather. Natalie and Blue already had towels out and were cranking tunes. The sun was out and it was a totally awesome June day. Summer was on its way.

I flopped down next to Natalie and helped myself to a chocolate chip cookie, courtesy of Natalie's mom. Blue's offerings would end up in the trash. Her mom's health food recipes weren't exactly yummy. "Can you believe school is almost out?"

"Less than three weeks," Natalie said. "I'm so excited." She was lying on her back wearing a tank top and shorts. "I can't wait for track to be over. I want to hang out and relax." She opened one eye. "I told my coach I was having female pain, which is why I'm not at practice today."

I grinned. "Way to go, Nat! I'm impressed."

"Was I going to miss out on enjoying this gorgeous afternoon? I couldn't bear to spend it sweating and getting dirty. I can run later, when it's dark." Natalie closed her eyes and held out her hands. "Sun, bake me, please."

"This is our last week of school," I said. The private schools got out way earlier than the public ones. "You guys still have three weeks left?"

"Don't you guys ever have to be in class?" Natalie grumbled.

"At least you have boys around," I said, stretching out beside her. How good did that warm sun feel? Heaven. I couldn't wait for L.A. "I'd trade a short school year for having boys around in a heartbeat."

"What good does the presence of boys do me? They only think of me as a friend. I'm one of the guys." It was Natalie's ongoing lament. As a runner, she was on coed teams all year long, but it hadn't done anything to help her social life. Which was okay with me. Now that Frances and Blue had boyfriends, Natalie and I had to support each other on Friday nights.

"I might have a solution to your boyfriend situation," Frances said.

I bit my lower lip and tried not to feel jealous, because I knew what Frances was about to offer.

"One of our teachers is hiring kids to work at a farm stand this summer," Frances said. "There will be boys and we earn money."

Natalie sat up. "Really?"

Frances nodded. "I'm going to sign up. Want to do it with me?"

7

"Yes!"

I frowned. "What about running camp? Aren't you going to running camp this summer?"

Natalie rubbed her chin. "Yeah, but only for a week in August." She looked at Frances. "Do you think he'd let me take off for a week to go to camp?"

"Definitely. He's totally cool."

I tried to imagine some hot, tanned guy rubbing sunscreen onto my back on an endless white beach. That would be so much better than hanging with my friends, hauling dirt piles around, right? Of course, right.

"I'm in," Blue said. "Sounds like fun."

I scrunched my eyes shut and thought about meeting Ashton Kutcher on the street and him asking me out. See? I wouldn't miss out by being away from my friends.

"Are you working at the farm stand too, Allie?" Frances asked.

I opened my eyes and put a big smile on my face. "I'm going to L.A. to visit my dad." How cool did that sound when I said it out loud? Yes, I had a dad who wanted to see me.

"I forgot." Blue sighed. "That's so awesome. I wish I was going with you."

"Me too," Natalie said.

WHO NEEDS BOYS?

By the time my friends finished discussing why L.A. was going to be so cool and how they were so bummed they couldn't go, I was feeling much better. Yeah, so they'd have a good time this summer without me. I'd have a good time too, and who knew? Maybe my dad would even ask me to live there with him. Maybe this was the first step to him wanting his daughter back in his life.

This was going to be the summer that changed my life. I was certain of it.

Three weeks later, I stood back and eyed all the stacks of clothes on my bed. No way were those going to fit in my two suitcases. I wondered if my mom had another one I could borrow. It was too late to go to the store and buy more luggage.

The advantage of having an absentee mom who was too busy dating to waste time on her daughter: the Guilt Credit Card. She figured she could buy my loyalty, and who was I to argue? She'd done well in the divorce, so I might as well have some benefit of the nightmare, don't you think? Of course, the credit card only worked when I could use it. At ten o'clock on a Friday night, there was nowhere I was going to find a suitcase for sale.

I stuck my head out into the hall. "Mom? Are you here?"

Silence.

The disadvantage of having an absentee mom: She was never around, Between dating and her career as an accountant, there wasn't a whole of time for mother/daughter things. We didn't even need the money due to the divorce settlement, but she said she needed the job for self-esteem purposes. Yeah, whatever.

I frowned as I wandered into her room to check under the bed for another suitcase. Should I call a cab for the airport tomorrow? She'd sworn she would be able take me, but she'd forgotten before. She'd even been squeezed out of the carpool circle with my friends.

After she left us at the movie theater at midnight, Blue's mom had decided that she'd take over my mom's duties.

Which was fine. Got us home, didn't it? And I had learned not to care that Mom wasn't home or didn't seem to give a rip if my head fell off and rolled out into the street. She'd just step over my beheaded body on her way out to her next date. Exactly how I liked it. I didn't need her. Which is why I was going to do everything in my power to convince my dad to invite me to stay out in L.A. with him. Yeah, sure, I'd miss my friends, but by the end of the summer I'd be dating Justin Timberlake and all his friends would be mine, and I'd have no room for missing my friends.

But first, I had to get all my cute clothes out to California with me, and that wasn't going to happen with my two small suitcases.

I dropped to my knees and peered under my mom's bed.

Nothing under the bed except dust and a pair of Ferragamos she'd discarded. Sadly, her feet were two sizes bigger than mine.

I checked her closet. Nothing. Time to try my sister's room.

I rifled through her stuff, but of course she'd taken her luggage with her when she'd gone off to London for a summer program to get her a step ahead before starting college in the fall. She had left behind a sweet black miniskirt and a lace camisole I'd been coveting for ages. Now they were mine!

Excellent. Wishing I had time to search for more lost treasures Louisa had left behind, I sighed as I walked out of her room clutching my new clothes. I really missed her. Yeah, she'd been out with her friends a lot over the last year, but she had been around to give me advice about boys or makeup or my friends.

And now she was in London getting educated. Or at least, that's what she'd said to my mom. I knew it was because she wanted to get out of this house, just like I did.

I stood in the upstairs hall and listened to the utter silence of the house. And to think I'd been upset I was missing out with my friends this summer. No way was hanging out with them worth enduring this tomb for three months, not when I had the option of going to L.A. with my dad.

Speaking of which, I really needed to find a duffel bag or something.

The front hall closet held nothing, and neither did the guest room. Darn it! There had to be something somewhere.

I walked to the kitchen and dialed my mom. I wasn't supposed to bother her on dates unless it was an emergency, but this definitely constituted an emergency, don't you think? Besides, she'd probably forgotten this was my last night at home and she'd appreciate the reminder so she could rush home and spend some quality time with me before I took off.

The phone rang and then went into voice mail.

So I dialed again. Same result. "Mom, call me as soon as you can."

Guess I was on my own to pack.

I kicked at the steps as I stomped back upstairs. Shouldn't someone want to see me off tonight? Shouldn't my mom be sad her daughter was leaving for three months? You'd think one night off from the dating scene wouldn't have killed her.

The doorbell rang before I made it to the top. "Mom?" Grinning, I ran down the stairs and flung it open. It was Natalie, Blue and Frances, their boyfriends, and pizza and soda and DVDs. Not as good as my mom, but also better than her. "What are you guys doing here?"

. "Farewell party for Allie, of course," Natalie announced. "You didn't think we were going to forget, did you?"

I couldn't wipe the grin off my face. "Maybe I did, a little." This was awesome! My true friends.

"Loser." Blue hugged me and then led the way inside. "To the family room," she announced. "That's where the surround sound is."

Theo, who was both Blue's older brother and Frances's boyfriend, slung his arm over my shoulder and hauled me into the living room. "You know we'll miss you."

I've known Theo since I was a baby. We'd all known each other forever, except for Colin, of course, Blue's boyfriend. But Colin was totally cool and fit in like he'd been one of the crew forever.

I was going to miss them. A lot. What if my dad didn't love me? What if I got out to L.A. and it was horrible?

Stephie Davis

"What's wrong?" Natalie slid next to me on the couch.

"Nothing." I looked around. "Where are the boys for me and Natalie?" I still hadn't figured out why Colin and Theo didn't bring their friends around for Natalie and me to try on for size. Probably because their friends were too cool to hang with a bunch of freshman girls. Well, forget that. I wasn't a freshman anymore. School was out, and I was on my way to being a sophomore.

Totally worthy of older boys. No, not boys. Guys. Men. Hot, sexy men who were waiting for me in L.A.

Colin grinned. "There were so many guys who wanted to come that we couldn't decide, so we decided not to bring anyone. But you girls were highly sought after."

"Yeah, right." I rolled my eyes and flopped back on the couch. "I'll have plenty of my own boys when I get to L.A." Then I sat up. "No, not boys. Men. I'll have men."

"You're only fourteen," Natalie pointed out. She was the only one who could talk about the age differential, since Blue and Frances were both dating older guys.

"Fifteen in a month. And I look like I'm eighteen." I shot a look at the boys. "Don't I?"

They exchanged wary glances, and I laughed. As if they'd go there with their girlfriends sitting next to them. Boys were so transparent. That's why I needed a man. A tanned California man.

Frances held up a DVD. "We got *The Sure Thing*. It's old, but it's about how much better California is than the ucky northeast, so we figured it would be good."

"Cool." I helped myself to a piece of pizza and tried not to be sad that I'd miss them. It was only for the summer. We'd be back together in the fall. Unless my dad asked me to stay. Right now, I almost didn't want to leave them. I mean, my friends were the only people in my life who would notice if I disappeared from the earth. Not only would they notice, but they'd care and actually try to find me. But maybe my dad was ready for that. He had invited me out for the whole summer, hadn't he? I sighed. It still didn't make it easier to leave my friends. "You guys won't, um, forget about me while I'm gone, will you?"

"No!" Blue flung her arms around me, and Natalie and Frances followed suit until I was being squashed underneath the pile. I screamed and hugged them back. And tickled them until we were all screaming. Somewhere between the elbows, I heard the phone ring.

"Someone get that. It's probably my mom calling back." As if I could get it. I was totally being pig-piled.

Then Theo interrupted the love fest. "It's your dad."

"My dad!" I scrambled free and grabbed the portable phone. "Dad?"

"How are you doing, hon?"

I walked into the living room and snuggled up on the couch. "I'm great. I'm almost finished packing. I can't wait." It was so good to hear his voice. I couldn't believe how long it had been since I'd seen him.

"Um . . . Allie . . ."

Something caught in my throat. "What's wrong?"

"Nothing's wrong. It's fine."

"What's fine?" I tucked my feet under a pillow and tried to keep my voice calm.

"It's Heidi."

"Your fiancée?" I thought of the gorgeous brunette my dad had e-mailed me a picture of last week. She looked way younger than my dad, but didn't everyone in California look young and beautiful?

"Yes. She's . . . ah . . . pregnant."

"Pregnant? I'm going to have a little sister or

brother?" Oh my gosh. That was so cool. A fresh start at a family. Yes! They'd totally need my help now! "You want me to be a nanny? I can totally do that. I'll watch her or him after school and . . ."

"Allie, hon, calm down."

"But this is cool! I can't wait to get out there. Will the baby be born this summer?"

"No, not until winter, but Heidi is really sick. The pregnancy isn't going well."

I frowned. "How sick?"

"Very sick. She's . . . ah . . . I don't think it would be a good idea for you to come out this summer."

My gut plummeted. "What?"

"I am going to have to take care of her, and she's on bed rest. Neither of us can be worrying about you."

I swallowed hard. "But I'm very independent. You don't have to worry about me at all. I can cook. I'll be your housekeeper. I'll take care of her while you're at work."

"I'm sorry, Allie. It will be too stressful. If things change, we'll call. Otherwise, can we take a rain check for next summer?"

"A rain check?" *A rain check?* "But I'm really easy. You won't even notice I'm there." I couldn't keep the tears out of my voice. "Dad?"

"I'm sorry, hon. It's just not the right time. I love

you, and I'll call you in a couple days. I have to run. Bye."

I sat there with the dial tone humming in my ear. I couldn't believe it.

No, I could believe it. I should have predicted it. How could I have been so stupid as to get my hopes up? After six years of excuses, you'd have thought I would have been smarter than that.

"Allie? You okay?" Frances was standing in the doorway, her face all scrunched up in concern.

I tossed the phone on the couch and smiled at her. "I have great news!"

"What?"

"I don't have to go to L.A.! I'm going to hang with you guys this summer. Isn't that great?" It was great. No way was I going to let my dad ruin my summer. Forget him. And next summer if he asked me back? *I'd* bail on *him* at the last second. Hah.

Frances frowned. "I thought you wanted to go to L.A."

"I was talking myself into it because I had to go. You know I was bummed to miss out on the farm stand thing." I swallowed hard and kept a grin on my face. "This will be great."

"But Mr. Novak said his staff was full. That there was no room."

For an instant, I felt my smile slip. What if I was

stuck at home all summer? In this horrible, empty house with no air-conditioning? Then I recovered. Mr. Novak was male. I could talk males into anything.

Except my dad apparently, but he wasn't male. He was a jerk.

"I'll call him." I headed for the kitchen and the phone book, delighted to find only three Sam Novaks. "There. I'll call each of them."

Frances's eyes were wide. "You're going to call him at home?"

"Of course. This is a crisis. I can't miss out on spending the summer with you guys." Plus, if I had to spend the entire summer alone I knew I would totally freak out. I decided to start at the bottom. A woman answered. "Is the Mr. Novak who lives there the one who teaches Latin?"

"Yes, it is. Who is this?"

I gave Frances the thumbs up. "One of his students. Can I talk to him?"

"He's not here. Can I take a message?"

Oh, wow. I hadn't thought of that. "Um . . . yeah . . . I was calling about the farm stand. I wanted to work for him."

"Sorry, sweetie, but it's full. You're the seventh person who has called him today, but there's no more space."

"But . . ." I was horrified by the tears that sprung to my eyes. I immediately spun around so Frances couldn't see. "You don't understand. All my friends are doing it."

"Then you should have signed up with them." Her voice was gentle, but unyielding.

"But I couldn't." I swallowed to crush the emotion rising in my throat. "I was supposed to go see my dad and he cancelled on me five minutes ago even though I've barely seen him in the last six years and he has this fiancée and I can't go and my mom's never home and I don't want to be alone all summer and . . ." I realized I was sobbing now, and I immediately shut my mouth.

Well, except for when I had to open it to suck in air. Heaving sobs were not the most dignified.

"What's your name?" The woman's voice was sympathetic and it made me want to start crying again. I hated sympathy. I was fine. Totally fine.

"Allie Morrison."

"What's your phone number?"

I gave it to her.

"I'll talk to Sam when he gets home, okay?"

"I have to be able to work there. I'll even do it for free. I'll do anything. I just can't stay here." How desperate did I sound? I never begged. Ever.

"He'll call you, but it might not be until tomorrow."

"Okay. I'll wait by the phone." I hung up and turned around. All my friends plus Colin and Theo were standing in the kitchen watching me.

I immediately wiped the tears off my cheeks and raised my chin. "I think we need to put in a different movie, don't you? I'm not feeling in a pro-California mood anymore."

Without waiting for a response, I grabbed a gallon of ice cream from the freezer and a spoon from the dish drainer and marched into the family room.

Mr. Novak had better not let me down.

Chapter Two

The call came on Sunday night. I'd been diving to the phone every time it rang all weekend, but all I'd had the pleasure of was marketing pitches for consolidating my student loans or getting a new mortgage, neither of which was high on my list of concerns.

Until eight fifty-one on Sunday night.

I grabbed the phone that had become my enemy and slammed it to my ear. "What?" I had deteriorated to hostile answering techniques to try to get the telemarketing people to hang up out of fear before starting their spiels. I had lost all hope that Mr. Novak would call me back. He was probably too afraid to let me down. Instead he was going to avoid facing me. Even more pathetic than my dad.

Adults suck.

"Allie? This is Mr. Novak."

Oh, *great*. Perfect timing for me to answer the phone with an attitude. "Hi. Sorry about how I answered the phone. I thought it was a telemarketer." I tried to squash the hope that surged in my chest. He was calling to tell me no, and I needed to prepare myself for it. I'd already decided that if he turned me down, I was going to use my guilt credit card and fly myself to London to live with Louisa. She'd understand that I couldn't stay here anymore, not without her *and* my friends.

"Kate talked to me."

"Kate?" Did I know a Kate?

"My wife. You spoke to her on Friday."

"Oh, right. Kate. She's very nice." His wife? It might be a little bit harder to win him over with my flirting if he was married. Not that I had the energy to flirt. I was too emotionally drained after having my heart explode every time the phone had rung for the last forty-eight hours. At first, I'd been hoping my dad would call back to say he'd changed his mind. Then I'd realized I was being stupid again and decided to settle for a call from Mr. Novak telling me I could work at the farm stand.

Then I'd finally decided that no one was going to call.

And now? I had hope again, which made me a fool.

"My staff is full, Allie."

It can't be! "But I have to do it. Please. I'll work for free and I'll do an awesome job and you won't regret it." See what hope does? Makes you beg. Makes you desperate. Makes you ashamed to be so pathetic.

I could hear Kate telling him something in the background. "It's not easy work," he said.

"So what?" Just because I wear cute outfits and have my nails done doesn't mean I can't do real work. At the very least, I was pretty sure I could get some of the boys to do it for me if I couldn't. I didn't want to go to London. I wanted to hang out with my friends. I *had* to get this job. "I can handle it, I promise. Please, please, please, please."

He covered the mouthpiece and I heard voices murmuring. Was Kate on my side? If so, I'd love her forever. After what felt like an eternity, he came back on. "Are you doing this for the boys or for the work?"

"The work. I have plenty of boys in my life." Well, not really. You could never have too many boys, and I wanted to do it so I could hang with my friends and meet boys, but I wasn't about to admit that to Mr. Novak. "I need to do something of value this summer." And I needed something, anything, to distract me from the fact that my dad had given me the ultimate rejection.

I hate my dad.

There was a long silence. "If you'll work hard, then you are welcome. If you slack off, I'll let you go."

All right! "Don't worry, Mr. Novak. I won't let you down." Yahoo! I couldn't wait to tell my friends!

"Tomorrow at seven-thirty."

Seven-thirty? I had to be at work at seven-thirty? This was summer. I was supposed to get up at ten o'clock in the morning, grab some OJ, then head to the beach to lie in the sun.

"Is there a problem with the hour?"

"No, not at all. I'll be there." I wasn't about to get myself fired after I'd had the job for only thirty seconds. "See you tomorrow."

I hung up and stared at the phone. This was the first job I'd ever had. I'd never even babysat before. Much as I was doing this for the boys and my friends, it looked like I was also going to have to work.

Which was fine.

How hard could it be?

Maybe if I was really successful and did a great

job, my parents would realize I actually had some value. Wouldn't that be a kicker?

On Monday, June twenty-fifth, I dressed with extra care for my first day of work. Carefully applied makeup, curled my hair so my new blond highlights accentuated my face. Painted my toenails and fingernails to match the melon-colored camisole I was wearing, and I chose my extra short white shorts. My new designer sandals were the perfect touch, and their open toes showed off my tanned feet perfectly. My mom's answer to the news that my dad had cancelled on me? Dropping me off at the mall to buy myself expensive things.

As much of a jerk as my dad was when he was around, he'd earned a ton of money as a surgeon. My mom scored in the divorce and I got the benefit of no parental supervision and all the funds I needed to entertain myself. Being the neglected offspring of divorced selfish jerks rocked.

Not that I was going to think about *him*. He had lost the right to occupy any of my thoughts.

My first day of work at Sam's Farm Stand. This summer was going to be great.

Blue's mom opened the door for me when I arrived at their house. "Hi, Allie! We're so glad you're coming." She inspected my outfit. "You're going to work in that?"

My friends appeared behind her. They were all wearing sneakers, jeans and T-shirts. And baseball hats—courtesy of Blue's mom and her skin-cancer warnings, no doubt. They each had a little backpack, which I assumed carried lunches their moms had packed.

I should have thought of that. I hoped I wasn't going to starve today. Apparently, there were some benefits to having a mom around to remember these things, but my mom had to be at work at seven, and she had an hour commute, so I never saw her in the mornings. She used to leave me notes and breakfast, but that hadn't happened in a long time.

Which was fine with me. I didn't need her.

"We're going to work on a produce farm," Frances said.

"Yeah, what's with that outfit?" Blue asked.

I frowned. "What's wrong with it?"

"You're going to ruin those sandals in the mud," Blue said.

I looked down at the sandals. They'd cost over a hundred dollars, and they looked good. High fashion, yet comfortable for a long day on my feet. "I think they'll be perfect."

"And your clothes are going to get filthy," Natalie said. As a cross-country runner, Natalie was the mud queen. Every day after practice she came in muddy, sweaty and grimy.

"So I'll wash them." I was one of those people who were gifted at being able to keep anything clean. Probably because I hated doing laundry and no one else was going to do it, so I tried to minimize the dirty clothes pile. "Let's go."

I followed my friends out to Blue's mom's Suburban, but she caught my arm. "Allie?"

Uh-oh. That was her Mom tone. "What?"

"Do you want to stay with us for the summer?"

I looked up. "Why?"

"Blue told me what happened with your dad. I don't want you to be alone at home if your mom isn't around, since Louisa is gone too."

I scowled, and swallowed the lump that had popped up in my throat. What was up with Blue telling her mom? I was fine. Why did everyone think I was upset? So my dad blew me off. So my mom was off dating instead of being a mom. So what? I didn't care. I liked having the house to myself.

Besides, now that Theo was dating Frances and Colin was dating Blue, going over to the Waller household actually made me feel more lonely. Even with my best friends, I was now an outsider.

"Thanks, but I'm okay. My mom's been busy lately, but she's around." I mean, I like Blue's parents and stuff, but they are always trying to pseudo-adopt me. I don't need to be adopted. I'm fine.

"Well, if you change your mind, let me know."

"Thanks." I climbed into the back of the Suburban and fell into a conversation about how many boys and of what age would be at the farm stand. Much more important stuff than discussing my need for a family, which was totally stupid.

Mr. Novak came out to greet us when Blue's mom drove into the dirt parking lot. He was wearing jeans and boots and a navy T-shirt with "Sam's Farm Stand" on the front. Sunglasses were perched on top of his head.

Was he hot or what? Drool-worthy.

Blue elbowed me. "This is your teacher? He's gorgeous."

"Yeah. Too bad he's married." And he was looking at me like he wasn't sure I should be there.

I immediately folded my arms across my chest and gave him my "I'm powerful so don't mess with me" look. It was almost the same as The Attitude, but the latter was for attracting boys, or more precisely, making them think you weren't sure whether you were going to speak to them, which of course, always made them want you. Mr. Novak wasn't my appropriate Attitude target seeing as how he was old, but it was important for him to know he'd hired someone who could withstand whatever he was going to throw at me. So I gave him some Attitude mixed with disdain. That should do it.

"I'm thinking I want to go to your school next year. I think I want to learn Latin," Blue whispered.

I grinned and tucked my arm through Blue's. "You have Colin. Isn't one older guy enough for you?"

"Or I could make do with that guy with the wheelbarrow." She nodded off to the right and I followed her glance.

A pretty cute guy was hauling a load of plants. He was wearing the same navy T-shirt as Mr. Novak, but didn't come close to filling it out the same way. Well, of course not. He looked like he was fifteen. A boy. Not a man. Cute though. Fending off his adoration would definitely be enough to heal my wounded ego after my dad's rejection.

"Welcome to Sam's," Mr. Novak announced. He looked at Blue's mom. "They'll be finished at three today."

Blue's mom nodded and then took off in the Suburban, no doubt to do some grocery shopping or something that normal moms do. She'd be back at five of three to pick us up. Blue's mom would never forget and leave us stranded.

Mr. Novak inspected each of us, a frown marking his brow when he came to my outfit. "Are those the only shoes you have?"

"Yes." Weren't they darling?

"You'll need sneakers tomorrow. Those will never work."

Well, I hadn't worn them to impress him. They were for the boys. So I tried to blind him with my smile instead and tried not to wonder if I'd already disappointed him.

He gave me a look, then turned to the rest of the crew. "I always pair up the newbies with some of my more experienced hands for the first month. I've already assigned you." He whistled and I saw the guy with the wheelbarrow head over.

Wow. Blue would freak if she got assigned to him.

The boy approached Mr. Novak. "What's up?"

Mr. Novak nodded at me. Wait a sec. Me? "Tad, this is Allie Morrison. Allie, this is Tad Simmons. You'll be Tad's right hand for the next month, Allie."

"But . . ." He was my age! I didn't hang out with guys who were my age. Especially with my less experienced friends currently dating high school graduates. If I was stuck with him, how was I going to meet the older ones? I needed to be paired with a *man*.

Tad didn't look any happier than I felt. "Are you kidding? Look at her. She'll be useless on a farm."

"Hey! I'm not useless." Did he think I couldn't hear or something? Just because I was wearing a cute outfit didn't mean I was incompetent. I always took care with my clothes because it was the best way to make people like me, and now he was using it as a reason not to like me?

I lifted my chin. No, it was impossible. I could totally succeed here, and Tad would like me and think I was cute.

"You're my best worker, Tad. I figure you'll be a good influence on Allie."

His best worker? So, was Tad going to be a spy to report back to Mr. Novak that I was useless and should be fired? No way. I wasn't going to lose this job. I was going to prove I was worth something. I narrowed my eyes and glared at Tad. "I'm perfectly capable."

Tad met my gaze, then took a deliberate look at my shoes. He didn't look impressed with my pedicure. I resisted the urge to curl my toes under and hide the rainbows painted on my big toenails.

"Rainbows." He sounded disgusted.

I scowled. "Don't judge me."

"I can see you two are going to get along well." Mr. Novak gave me a little push toward Tad. "I think there might be a pair of old boots in one of the barns. See what you can find, Tad."

He scowled. "I don't have time to be finding her boots. We have work to do."

"Find the boots."

Tad folded his arms across his chest and glared at me.

What was his problem? What had I done to him? He hated me because my toes matched my shirt? Most boys would have liked it and given me a nice smile and been excited to be paired with me.

But not the idiot over there. Which was fine. He was a boy, and who needed boys? I needed an older guy. At least seventeen, preferably in college.

Yes, that was the problem. He was too young to appreciate me. See? Everything would be okay.

"Fine. Come on." He turned away without waiting to see if I followed. What? He thought he was too good for me? It was so the other way around. I didn't need him and I didn't care what he thought of me.

"You better hustle. It'll be hard to run in those shoes and Tad's not going to wait." Mr. Novak then turned back to my friends and corralled them so he could herd them off to their new partners.

Leaving me standing there in the dirt parking lot like an idiot.

Tad stopped at the edge of the parking lot and turned around. "Are you coming?"

Did I have a choice? I lifted my chin and stalked toward him, detouring around two mud puddles. I was so not going to ruin my sandals before a cute older guy had a chance to compliment me on them. Because there was nothing wrong with me or how I looked and some guy was going to notice it even if I had to shove strawberries up his nose to get him to appreciate me.

I could have sworn Tad was laughing at me by the time I reached him, but his face was stoic. Except one corner of his mouth, which was twitching. All I can say is he better be leering at my boobs and not finding amusement at my expense.

Between my dad and my mom and her obsession with dating, I had very little tolerance for the opposite sex these days, and I wasn't going to be taking any grief from this one. Besides, he was my age! A mere boy!

I followed Tad behind the farm stand, stepping around piles of dirt and mud. Shoes and pedicure were still intact, although I'd almost stepped in a pile of something nasty when I'd looked up to smile at a cute guy who was hauling some hoses past me.

Tad stepped into a barn that was full of hoses, crates and other farm-type equipment. "There's a lost and found in the back. The boots must be in there."

It smelled like dust and mold and stale air. Yuck.

Tad pulled open a creaky wooden door in the back, then disappeared inside a small room that looked it might have stored feed or something, if all the bins built into the walls were any indication. From the peek I got, it looked like my mom's attic. Dirty, old, farm implements piled all over the place. Total yuck. I opted to wait outside. No need to go diving into some rat haven. I mean, I was totally capable of handling it, but there was no need to tread on his ego by insisting I go in instead of him.

Even though I wasn't remotely interested in impressing him, he was still a boy and it was important to keep my Boy Allure on high so I could turn it on when I met a guy I was interested in. You think it's luck that boys all want to kiss me? No way. I work very hard at projecting the right attitude.

See, it's like this: You have to pretend not to like

them while shooting them flirty glances. And you have to always be aware of their ego and treat it carefully—unless they do you wrong, in which case you stomp mercilessly all over it and leave them behind to curl up and die a painful death of mourning for the girl they couldn't have. It takes skill and commitment, and I might as well practice on Tad, even though I didn't care if he liked me.

Actually, that's the trick. You can't care too much. It's good to have boys like you. But I always keep them at a distance; I never give them the chance to hurt me. Kiss them, flirt with them, and keep them on a string, but never, ever fall for one.

That's my cardinal rule. I would never break it. And if I had any doubts, the incident with my dad provided adequate reinforcement for why I would never let myself care what a guy thought of me. Especially someone like Tad, who was a mere boy and not worth my time, let alone my angst.

He emerged from a pile of crusty old clothes, blankets and shoes holding a pair of dirty, worn hiking boots that looked about four sizes too big for me. "Here you go." He dropped them at my feet.

"You're kidding." It was one thing to borrow clothes from my sister or my friends, but those boots were gross. There was mud all over them, and they were wrinkled and smelled like something had died in them.

"You'll be glad to have them."

First of all, there was no way I was putting my feet in there, especially without socks. Second, my sandals were perfectly fine. They were comfortable and I could stand all day in them. Unlike those monstrosities. "I'll pass." Besides, if I looked awful, then there'd be nothing left to appeal to anyone. I wasn't ready to be an outcast.

"Suit yourself." He walked off without another look back.

Yeesh. What was his problem?

Useless. That was his problem. He thought I was useless.

Well, forget him. My parents might not think I was worth noticing, and there was nothing I could do about that—not that I cared—but I sure didn't have to be dismissed by some fifteen-year-old jerk. I was going to work with him, and he was going to like it.

Please note, however, that I wasn't trying to get him to *like* me. I was merely going to prove he was wrong. Big difference.

I ran across the barn floor and settled in next to him. "What's on the agenda for today?"

"Carrots."

Carrots? I could totally handle carrots. I chopped those things up for salad all the time. "Cool."

He shot me a look, and I shot one right back. "I'm not incompetent."

He lifted a brow, but said nothing.

Jerk.

Tad pointed at a little shed. "In there is a wheelbarrow. Grab it, and a couple tools for digging." He looked at my hands. "I don't suppose you have work gloves."

I shoved my manicure in my pockets. "No."

"There might be a pair in there. If not . . ." He shrugged. "You'll need to get those nails redone tonight."

He didn't make it sound like a compliment. Never had anyone made me feel stupid for trying to look nice before.

I wasn't all that fond of it.

I was really going to enjoy making him feel like a fool for misjudging me.

"After you get the wheelbarrow and stuff, head to that field back there. I'll be out there and I'll show you what to do." He pointed to a spot that was three fields over. It was a gorgeous sunny day, but there was no breeze and that field looked hot. Really hot.

Tomorrow I was bringing a water bottle. Today?

I'd die of thirst before I'd ask Tad for a drink from his. A girl had to find pride where she could. "Fine. I'll be right out."

He nodded, picked up his wheelbarrow and headed off.

For an instant, I was tempted to go over to the farm stand building and hide from Tad and his disapproving looks.

Except Mr. Novak was in there, and he'd know I'd failed if I went in.

Failure was not an option. It would mean I'd be stuck in my empty house all summer with nothing to do and no one to talk to.

No, thanks. Even Tad was better than that. So I pulled open the door to the shed and walked inside, smacking right into the hottest guy I'd ever seen. "Oh, sorry." Tall, broad shoulders, short dark hair and a nice smile. And he had to be at least eighteen. I bet he was in college. Certainly not some fifteen-year-old like Tad the Jerk.

He had a smile, and he was directing it at me. It felt like forever since anyone had smiled at me. I flashed him my best smile. "I'm Allie."

He shook my hand and gave me a wink. "Rand. You new?"

"Does it show?"

He grinned again, and I noticed he had dimples. "You're clean. It's always a sign of a newbie."

Rand didn't make being clean sound like an insult. I loved him for that. "I have to go work with carrots. I don't think the clean thing will survive that." Though I was going to make every effort to make sure it did. No need to ruin my clothes for the sake of some veggies.

He gave me a sympathetic look. "I saw you're with Tad, huh?"

"I'm not *with* him. I'm working with him is all."

Rand lifted his brow. "Thanks for the clarification."

Aha. So he'd caught my drift. I'd wondered if he was going to pick that up. Good to know at least one guy on this farm had some sense when it came to girls. I flipped him a grin. "Anytime." Time to make him yearn for me. Leave while he's still wanting more. "So, I'll just grab my stuff and head out." I turned to the shelf full of digging utensils, stared at the selection for a minute, and then my brain began to hurt. I had no idea what I was supposed to use for carrots.

Rand picked up several tools and set them in my hand. "Try these."

I actually felt tears in the back of my throat. How

pathetic was I? Just because someone was actually being nice to me, I had to cry? Totally uncool and it needed to stop right now!

Rand picked up my empty hand and turned it over. If he made a mean comment about my manicure, I was going to kick him in the shin, I really was. "You have gloves?"

I shook my head. "I didn't know I was supposed to bring any."

"Your hands will get destroyed." He pulled out a set that had been hanging from his back pocket. "Use mine."

I stared at them. "You're giving me yours? What about your hands?"

"I'll be fine. I have easy stuff today." He held them out. "They'll be huge on you, but they'll protect you."

Why couldn't I be paired with Rand? He was perfect. But no. I was stuck with Tad the Toadhead. "Thanks."

He nodded, then tossed a couple wooden crates in the wheelbarrow. "You'll need some of these."

Nice of Tad to tell me. He was probably hoping I'd show up with all the wrong things so he could keep sending me on the three-field trek back to the shed to retrieve items. Probably wanted to break my spirit before the first day was out.

Hah. Fat chance of that. First of all, no one was going to break me. Second of all, I had my secret weapon in Rand.

"All set?"

I grinned and picked up the wheelbarrow, and promptly tipped it over. Before I could even feel stupid, Rand picked it back up for me. "You need to wrap your thumbs around the handle like this." He set my hand on the wooden handle and moved my thumb to the side. "That gives you more stability."

His hand was about three times the size of mine. A total man. I was going to melt right there. I didn't even have to flirt to get him to be nice to me. He just was. I managed a weak smile. "Thanks." Yeesh. Did I have any other word in my vocabulary besides thanks? I sounded like a dork. "Any more tips?"

He laughed. "Many more, but I don't want to overwhelm you. I'll dole them out in pieces."

Did that mean he was going to make sure we ran into each other from time to time? I could deal with that. I hoped he stopped by when I was with Tad. Let Tad know what he was missing. "Sounds good. If you hear me scream, you'll know I'm in need of one of your tips." And I was using the word "tips" loosely to include advice, a smile and a generally warm fuzzy feeling.

"Tad's probably getting testy," I said.

"Yeah." He looked like he wanted to say something. "How old are you?"

I hesitated. I could say fifteen, and it would almost be true, but would that be too young? "How old do you think I am?"

He cocked his head. "Seventeen?"

"Close enough. And you?"

"Seventeen for another few weeks."

And I'd be fifteen in another few weeks. So that was only a three-year difference. Worked for me. "I'll see you around. Thanks again."

He nodded and walked me to the door.

I felt him watching me all the way out to the field. It was hard to have a seductive walk when tromping through a field wearing sandals and pushing a wheelbarrow, but I did my best. A girl has to have priorities.

Chapter Three

I found Tad on his hands and knees hauling carrots out of the dirt. "Hi."

He sat back on his heels. "What took you so long?"

The happy Rand feeling dissipated. "It took me a while to find everything. You didn't tell me I needed crates."

He rubbed his glove over his chin, leaving a black smudge of dirt. I decided not to tell him. Besides, he probably thought it was a fashion statement.

"I can't remember everything," Tad said. "I expect you to be able to fend for yourself at least a little bit."

"Isn't it your job to remember everything? It's not my fault I'm new, and Mr. Novak says you're some superstar, so I figure he probably *does* expect you to remember everything." I folded my arms across my chest. I could already feel sweat dripping down my back from the heat. "I'm not a loser, Tad."

He looked surprised. "I never said you were a loser."

"You didn't need to. It's obvious what you think of me." I swallowed and tried to force away the bad feeling. Since when did I let anyone's opinions of me hurt? If I started doing that, between my dad and my mom, I'd never be able to get out of bed in the morning. If I could survive them, Tad was no problem.

So why was I so upset? Probably residual from the L.A. thing. Big mistake to let my dad have that much power. There would be no more of that. Time to focus on the present, which was keeping my job. "So, what do I do?"

Tad stuck his mini-shovel into the dirt and stood up. "Come this way."

Manhandling my wheelbarrow over the lumpy ground, I trailed behind Tad. I'd bet Rand would have offered to take the wheelbarrow for me, not that I needed help or anything, but I wouldn't be averse to a little show of common decency.

The wheelbarrow hit a rut and flipped over, dumping my empty crates, my tools and my gloves onto the field.

Tad didn't even notice. He just kept walking.

I hate you!

He didn't hear my mental curse, and I managed to right my load before he turned around. "Coming?"

I said nothing, just leaned into the wheelbarrow and shoved it across the field.

He took me almost thirty yards away from where he was working, then he stopped. "Here."

I dropped the wheelbarrow and looked at my hands. They were burning and there were red spots at the base of my fingers. Blisters already? Rand wasn't kidding about the gloves. Guess they should be on my hands instead of taking up space in my wheelbarrow, huh?

Tad dropped to his knees. "Watch."

I looked at the dirt and then at my white shorts and decided to stand.

He stuck a little shovel into the dirt and did this wiggly thing while tugging on a green leafy part, then a bunch of carrots popped out of the dirt. Cool. He shook off the dirt, wrapped a tie around the leafy part, then set the bundle in a crate. "Got it?"

"No problem." Didn't look very hard.

"Good." He pointed down the row. "Finish this row and then check in with me."

The row? It was like seventeen miles long. It

would take me all day to drive that far, let alone crawl along pulling carrots out of the ground.

Tad eyed me. "Problem?"

I wrinkled my nose at him. "Sorry to disappoint you, but no, I'm fine."

"You think I want you to have a problem?" He handed me the shovel. "Believe me, I would be thrilled if you became self-sufficient within five minutes. Taking care of someone who doesn't want to get dirty isn't what I'm here for."

I grabbed the shovel. "I get dirty."

"Do you? Your shorts look pretty white to me."

I glared at him and sat down in the field, white shorts and all.

He lifted a brow. "Tomorrow you should wear jeans or get knee pads. Your knees will be hashed from kneeling in the fields all day."

Again, so nice of someone to tell me this ahead of time. I wondered if Rand had a spare pair of knee pads on him. "I'll be fine."

He shrugged. "If you need me, yell."

Ha. I'd let myself get bitten by a rattlesnake before I'd admit to Tad that I needed help.

Ten hours later I looked at my watch. Then I shook it and looked at it again. Had it stopped? According to my watch, I'd only been working for thirty minutes. Impossible. I was melting from the heat, my muscles were aching, my knees were killing me and I was so thirsty I kept expecting to shrivel up into a pile of dust. Rand's gloves were so huge that every time I tried to grab something, the fingers folded over on the ends and got all tangled up.

But when I tried to ditch the gloves, I totally mangled my hands. So the gloves were on and I was exhausted.

I tossed another bundle into the crate and inspected my progress. Six? I'd pulled out only six?

I sat back on my heels and looked across the field. Tad had moved much farther down the field and there were carrot bunches flying through the air in rapid succession. He had headphones on and was whistling. Whistling. How could he be whistling? This was torture of the worst kind.

"Allie!"

My heart catapulted out of my body, and I screeched and jumped up, only to find Natalie standing behind me laughing. "You scared me!"

"Sorry." She dropped a crate in the next row and then fell to her knees. "They're short on carrots, so I get to help you." Natalie was wearing jeans and knee pads, and she had on a set of new gloves that fit her hands. She also had a water bottle on her hip.

"How did you know to bring all that stuff?"

"What stuff?" She looked cheerful and happy, and her cheeks were already flushed from the sun.

"The knee pads and gloves."

"Oh. It was in Mr. Novak's e-mail last week."

An e-mail that I hadn't gotten because I hadn't been signed up at the time. Nice.

On the other hand, at least I didn't have to take it personally anymore. It was merely the price of being late to the party.

Natalie started tugging at a bunch of carrots. "So, you have a cute guy, huh? Is he nice?"

"He's a jerk." I watched Natalie's technique and tried to mimic it. "How'd you get it out so easily?"

"You have to give it a little twist." She showed me, but I still couldn't recreate it. So she came over to my row and showed me exactly where to put my hands and how to twist.

"Like that?"

"Almost." She aimed my shovel for me. "Just put this here like that and . . . voilà."

"Nice job."

We both looked up to find Tad standing over us. The sun made the red highlights in his light-brown hair stand out. I paid good money for highlights like that, and he just had them. I was so sure he didn't appreciate them.

"I'm Tad."

Since I already knew him, I guessed the intro wasn't for my benefit.

Natalie stuck her dirty gloved hand at him, and he shook it. "Natalie Page. Allie's friend."

Tad glanced at me, then back at Natalie, and I knew he was wondering what we could have in common. What? Because Natalie was so much cooler than me? Since when did Natalie get the attention of boys instead of me?

Since dirt and harvesting carrots became important, apparently.

"You're new, aren't you?" Tad asked.

Natalie nodded. "First day."

"How'd you learn how to do the carrots?"

She shrugged. "I figured it out. Not too hard." She tossed a bundle into her crate. "They ran out of carrots at the stand, so they sent me out here to help."

A look from Tad said that if I was faster, they wouldn't have needed to give me help.

How unfair was that? I was trying!

"Thanks for your help," Tad said. And then he smiled at her.

Smiled!

I didn't even think his mouth went in that direction, and Natalie got a smile?

She grinned back. "No problem. It's fun."

I stared at Natalie. "You think this is fun?"

"Sure. Better than running up hills for two hours on a hot day."

Tad looked curious. "You're a runner?"

"Yep. Cross country and track."

"Want to run sometime after work?"

"Sure. Not today, because I don't have my running shoes. Tomorrow?"

Tad nodded. "Sounds good. Nice to meet you, Natalie." Without even glancing in my direction, he walked back across the field to his wheelbarrow.

"He sure seems nice," Natalie said. "Why is he a jerk?"

I stared after him. "He doesn't treat me like that."

"Like what?" Two more bundles of carrots hit the crate.

"Like a human being."

"Really?" Natalie rested her hands on her hips and watched him walk away. "What's he doing?"

"Being mean." I swallowed and realized I sounded pathetic. "I mean, he's treating me like I'm some prima donna who doesn't want to work hard, like I'm keeping him from more important things."

Natalie shot me a look. "Well, you did go pretty heavy on the makeup today, and that outfit isn't exactly what most people would pick to go work in the fields." She held up her hand before I could protest. "I know you work hard, but can you blame someone for getting the wrong impression?"

I was not in the mood to give Tad the benefit of the doubt.

"Who knows? Maybe his poor heart was broken by some gorgeous girl who didn't think working in the fields was dignified enough, and now he has a crush on you already, but he's too wounded to believe there's any hope, so he's trying to push you away before you can break his heart."

Despite my best efforts to continue to feel sorry for myself, I laughed. "Or maybe he's just a jerk."

"Maybe. But I think he has the hots for you."

I grabbed a green tuft and wedged my shovel in. "No way. I can tell when guys have the hots for me. They flirt, they smile, and they try to win me over by being nice. Tad definitely thinks I'm a loser." I glared at his back across the field. *And I'm not a loser, for your information.*

"He doesn't think you're a loser." Natalie lifted a

brow at my rolled eyes. "You want to make a bet on it?"

I glanced at Natalie, who was already on to her second crate. "What are you talking about?"

"I bet you can get him."

"First of all, you're the one he wants to go running with. Second, I don't pursue guys. They come after me or I move on." Translation: If I cared enough about a guy to pursue him, then he could hurt me. If I treat guys as trinkets that I could care less about, then I'm the one in the power seat, right? Chasing after Tad would put me in a way vulnerable position, even if it was merely for a bet.

No way.

Natalie rolled her eyes and tossed three bundles of carrots in my crate. "All guys want to run with me. I'm a buddy. A friend. Not a girl. Doesn't mean he wants me."

"Well, maybe you want him. I'm not getting between you two."

Natalie stopped pulling and stared at me. "You're afraid."

"Afraid? Me? You have to be kidding." I wasn't afraid of anything or anyone. "Afraid of what?"

"Of Tad. Of getting rejected." She tapped my thigh with her shovel. "I don't want him. He's a runner, and I don't date runners. They sweat and get dirty and remind me of track practice. So that argument doesn't fly."

I jabbed my shovel into the dirt. Hard. *I hate this!*

"You're afraid you've met your match in Tad."

"I am not. I could have him if I wanted." But I didn't want him, any more than I wanted my dad. Okay, so I really did want my dad. But I was working on that, and I'd certainly learned my lesson. There would be no yearning for boys who didn't adore me from the first moment. "But why bother? There are other guys around who are better options. Like Rand. Have you met Rand? He let me borrow his gloves." Unlike Tad, who didn't even tell me about the crates.

"Rand? Haven't met him. Is he a runner?"

I managed to distract Natalie into a discussion of Rand's merits, but I hadn't forgotten about our conversation. I kept sneaking glances over at Tad, who was moving farther and farther away as he powered through the carrots. Natalie would probably be able to keep up with him, except she kept putting her carrots in my crate. A true friend, despite the fact that she thought Tad would be a good match for me.

No way was I going to ruin my summer by obsessing about a guy who didn't want me.

So there.

* * *

I collapsed in the back of Blue's mom's Suburban at three o'clock. I closed my eyes, let my head flop against the seat and prayed the farm stand would burn down between now and tomorrow morning.

My friends were busy chattering. How was that possible? Weren't they exhausted?

Then I heard Blue mention a cash register and I sat up. "You're working the register?"

She nodded. "I'm in training, actually. I only get to be on duty when it's quiet. Otherwise, I help Frances stock the shelves."

"Stock shelves? You mean you carry stuff from the back room into the store?"

"Yep. Do you have any idea how many cute guys there are working here?" Blue sighed. "It's almost enough to make a girl wish she didn't have a boyfriend."

"So many? I saw two. Or one, rather. One cute one and one jerk. I spent the rest of the day chatting with dirt and carrots."

"You also chatted with a cute guy named Tad," Natalie chimed in.

Unfortunately, she was in the seat in front of me so I couldn't kick her. I made a mental note to remember to do it later.

Frances was sitting next to me, and she tapped me on the shoulder. "Spill."

"Yeah." Blue turned around and leaned over the back of the seat. "How come we're halfway home and we haven't heard about Tad?"

"Because he's a jerk."

Natalie shook her head. "I think he's madly in love with her and he doesn't know what to do about it."

"No chance." Rand on the other hand, I wouldn't argue. Not that he loved me, but he at least realized I wasn't carrying rabies.

Blue looked amused. "I don't know. Colin never had the hots for Allie. It does happen."

"Thanks . . . I think."

"Same with Theo," Frances said. "He even said he's not sure why so many guys are in love with you."

Okay, so I wasn't really digging this turn of the conversation, even if they were agreeing with me in some bizarre way by stating that it was very possible Tad didn't like me. "I never wanted Colin or Theo."

"So it was mutual," Blue said.

"Maybe you didn't want them because you realized they didn't want you," Frances suggested. "A subliminal defense mechanism."

I stared at her. "What are you, a psychiatrist?"

"I'm thinking about it. Good idea, huh? Of course, that means medical school. My parents are beside themselves with glee at the thought of their daughter being a doctor." Frances rolled her eyes. "They're so weird."

She was so wrong. It wasn't a defense mechanism. I hadn't liked them. If I had, I could have had them. But I didn't.

Natalie seemed to be of the same mind I was. "So, you're saying that there are boys who are immune to Allie?"

Frances and Blue both nodded. "Absolutely."

Natalie grinned. "Wanna bet?"

I dragged my weary body into a fighting stance. "Not this again. No bet."

"What bet?" Blue asked.

"Allie and I will bet that Allie can win Tad over by the end of the summer. You two seem to think that there are boys who are immune, so I'm guessing you two would bet that she couldn't get him interested in her."

"Natalie, that's a stupid idea. I'm not going to pursue Tad." Despite what Natalie thought, he really didn't like me, and I never wasted my time on guys who didn't like me. Not because I couldn't eventually win them over, but why bother when there were plenty of others who required no effort?

Blue and Frances huddled up and whispered behind their hands while I glared at Natalie. "I'm not doing a stupid bet."

The twosome broke formation. "Okay, here's the deal. We know that some boys aren't into Allie, but we need to inspect this Tad guy first and see if he qualifies. We're not going to make a bet over some guy who has already asked her out."

I snorted. "Trust me, Tad's not going to ask me out, unless it's into the street in front of an oncoming car." Frances and Blue lifted their eyebrows, and I scowled. "I'm not taking this bet. No way. Boys are about entertainment, not bets."

They all ignored me, setting up plans for Blue and Frances to inspect the interaction between me and Tad tomorrow.

How completely humiliating. A bet to see exactly how unappealing I actually was. There was no way I could let that happen. I did not want to be in a position of trying to force some guy to like me. Like I didn't have enough rejection in my life already.

Tad was history. Rand was what I needed.

Actually, what I really needed were knee pads, a water bottle and a pair of work gloves. After I found a way to get myself to the mall tonight to buy them, I'd think about tackling Rand.

And I was *not* going to think about Tad or my dad or anything.

Work gloves and Rand. The stuff of fantasies.

Chapter Four

Tad was loading up his wheelbarrow when I found him in the supply shack the next morning. I was wearing jeans and I had all my supplies, courtesy of a cab ride to the mall. Mom hadn't been around and my friends' parents had opted not to do car-pool duty.

No problem. That's why my mom left me cash when she went out. Guilt money.

I was wearing a cute pink T-shirt and a pair of sneakers that were practical, but still very trendy. I decided my makeup had been right yesterday, so I did the same thing and fixed my hair.

The perfect combination of cute and ready to work hard. Tad would see the error of his ways. "Hi, Tad."

He glanced up and inspected my outfit. Then he nodded. "Better."

Better? That's all he could say? No lingering inspection at all? Just "better"?

"Don't you have a Sam's T-shirt?"

My T-shirt rocked. The V neck showed off my cleavage, and the fitted waist showed my curves. And he wanted me to put on that shapeless navy bag?

Blue and Frances walked into the shed, squawking with completely fake surprise. "Oh my gosh, we didn't realize anyone was in here."

I scowled at them, but Tad looked amused. Amused. Why did they amuse him and I disgusted him?

Frances and Blue quickly introduced themselves to Tad, and he was friendly back. Until they said they were friends with me, at which point his demeanor changed. Not a lot. But I saw his eyes flick in my direction again.

"What? Are they too normal to be friends with me?" I snapped.

Tad looked surprised. "What?"

"Every time you meet one of my friends, you give me a look like, how come you're hanging out with someone who's normal? What is so wrong with me?" I couldn't take it anymore. I was so uncomfortable with someone not liking me, especially someone I had to work with.

Tad glanced at my friends, then back at me, then shifted his weight to his left foot. Then back to his right foot. *Am I making you nervous?* Good. "There's nothing wrong with you."

"No? Then why the hostility?"

Tad looked even more uncomfortable. "I'm not hostile."

"You certainly aren't like Rand is."

"Rand?" His eyes narrowed. "You want me to be like Rand?"

"He at least seems to think I have some value, and he doesn't expect me to be an expert on farm work on my first day."

Tad shrugged. "Feel free to request that you get switched to him."

Yeah, right. As if I could afford to make Mr. Novak question his last-minute decision to add me to the staff. And why didn't Tad care if I left him?

Because he was a jerk, and I wasn't going to care about it.

Blue swung her arm around my shoulder. "Looks like we're on. You and Natalie versus Frances and me."

"I'm not doing it."

"Good luck. Terms will be negotiated on the ride home." Frances grinned at Tad. "Have a good day, you two."

I tried to melt them with my glare, but they sauntered out of the shed without so much as a wobble.

Leaving me alone with Tad. What was I supposed to say?

"Ready?"

I looked at him standing there with his supplies, and realized he was cute. Not cute like Rand, but cute, like he should be nice and make me smile. I wanted him to smile at me. Just once. Because he meant it.

He furrowed his eyebrows and looked at me. "What?"

"Nothing." I picked up my supplies and dumped them in the wheelbarrow. "Where to?"

"Tomatoes."

Great. I love tomatoes.

I hate tomatoes. I hate those stupid stakes and those little ties and that stupid fertilizer and the murderous hose and everything about a stupid farm. I'd been working side by side with Tad for two weeks, and nothing had improved. He was still annoyed to be stuck with me, I wasn't getting the hang of this farming business, and I'd done no more than exchange a few flirting comments with

Rand, who seemed to be working on a different part of the farm.

So basically, my summer sucked so far.

At the moment, I was lying on my back staring up at the blue sky, having tripped myself with the hose. Water was currently shooting up the left side of my jeans, turning my resting place into a deep puddle of mud, and I didn't care.

I was done.

With any luck, the mud would turn into quicksand and I would slowly sink below the earth and find peace.

My sun turned to shade and Tad loomed over me. "You okay?"

"Fine. I'm taking a break."

"In the mud?"

"I was too clean."

He laughed and held out his hand. "I'll help you up."

I frowned. "Why are you being nice?" No doubt, he had some ulterior motive for that offer to haul me out of the mud. The morning had confirmed my suspicions of yesterday and every day before that: Tad thought I was an idiot, he didn't respond to my appearance, and he was annoyed as all get out that he was stuck with me. So the last thing I was going to believe was that he actually wanted to pull me out of the mud.

His smile faded and he let his hand drop. "You really think I'm mean?"

"To me." The mud was gooshing around me and I realized how stupid I was being. As if lying in mud solved any of my problems.

"Allie!" Rand appeared next to Tad. "What happened?"

There was genuine concern on his face, so I smiled. "I had a fight with the hose. I lost."

"I guess." Without waiting for consent, he grabbed me under the arms and pulled me to my feet. What a guy. Taking charge to rescue me. That's what I needed. "You're a mess."

"Thanks." Nice of him to point that out, seeing as how he was one of the cute guys who I actually wanted to impress, and still had a chance of impressing. My makeup must still be intact if he was being nice.

"No, in a cute way."

Tad rolled his eyes and made some annoyed noise. I considered sticking my tongue out at him, but decided to rise above it. He then retrieved the hose. "Turn around."

I stared at the gushing water. "You're going to hose me off?"

"You want to stay muddy all day?"

"Well, no, but . . ." I looked at Rand. Was this normal operating procedure? Rand looked amused. Was I being made fun of or was this legit? I'd never felt so unsure of myself around boys before. It was all my dad's fault. He'd totally screwed me up.

At that moment, Natalie walked around the corner carrying a basket of corn. She took a quick assessment of the situation, then dropped the basket and walked over. "You going to hose her off?"

Tad raised a brow. "Hey, Natalie."

She nodded. "Get me too. I'm broiling." She stood next to me and put her arm around my shoulder. "Have at it."

"Um . . . Nat?" She gave me a wink and turned us around so our backs were to the boys.

The cold water knocked the breath out of me, and I saw Natalie's mouth snap open in shock. After a moment, she grinned at me. "Fun, huh?"

"Fun?"

She leaned closer, bracing herself against the onslaught of water hitting our backs. "You're on a farm. You need to loosen up and have some fun. Show Tad that you're more than a manicure and expensive sandals."

"I'm not doing this for Tad," I muttered, spitting

out a mouthful of water when the stream hit my face. I was pretty sure I heard a couple of male snickers.

"The bet is on with Blue and Frances," Natalie said. "And I hate to lose. So you *will* do as I say." She raised her voice. "You guys seem to be having fun." She lowered her voice as they laughed again. "Take the hose and squirt them back."

"What? No . . ."

She turned us around, and we both got a faceful of water. Rand was holding the hose now, and he was looking thoroughly entertained. Tad was standing next to him, looking unsure. Probably afraid I was going to attack him or something.

Natalie elbowed me, and I saw that the hose was on the ground next to my foot. It would be so easy to grab it out of Rand's hands before he realized what was going on. I looked at Tad, and felt no inspiration. Then I saw the amusement on Rand's face and I knew that this was no longer about mud.

Forget Tad. I was in this for Rand.

So I pretended to tie my shoe—got a headful of water in the process—then I grabbed the hose and gave it a hard yank.

It immediately flew out of Rand's hand. Natalie dove on it and we both aimed it right at the boys. Well, I was aiming for Rand and Natalie was aiming for Tad, so they both got a full frontal dose of water. Rand howled, and I started laughing. He looked so outraged it was hilarious.

Even Tad was laughing a little bit. Didn't mean I liked him or anything.

"What's going on out here?" Mr. Novak's shout was enough to make us drop the hose instantly.

I wiped my soggy hair out of my eyes and pulled my wet shirt away from my body. "I fell in the mud and they were hosing me off."

Mr. Novak looked at the wet group and I thought I saw the corner of his mouth twitching. "Did *all* of you fall in the mud?"

Natalie grinned. "Just Allie. The rest of us were screwing around."

Natalie! I stepped on her foot and glared at her. She was so going to get us busted.

But Mr. Novak had eyes only for Tad. "You disappoint me."

The laugher faded from his eyes and he looked annoyed again. Hey! It wasn't my fault. "She was muddy. I was just hosing her off."

Natalie was still dripping, and Tad and Rand were soaked. I wondered if my makeup had run all over my face. Either that or it was totally gone. Either way, I wasn't exactly a fashionista anymore.

Mr. Novak lifted a brow. "Save the water fights

for after hours, okay? Hosing off is fine. Anything more? Not. Got it?"

We all nodded, and I tensed myself waiting for him to fire me. All he needed was an excuse to send me packing.

"Well, get back to work." Mr. Novak gave us a stern look that was softened a little by a certain gleam I detected in his eyes. "And all of you have to work out back today. You'll scare the customers."

That's it? I wasn't in serious trouble? I looked at Natalie, who was grinning even as water dripped from her chin. "Well, I feel much better now. No longer in danger of melting," she announced. "Appreciate the hosing, guys."

She picked up her basket of corn. "See you guys around."

"Are we still running after work?" Tad asked.

"Yep." She gave me a wink. "See ya."

She left me with Rand and Tad. Rand made a face at me. "I can't believe you squirted me."

Back in my comfort zone. Flirting with a guy. "Am I too much for you?"

He lifted a brow. "Not a chance. Got plans for Friday?"

Tad narrowed his eyes and turned away to begin rolling up the hose.

"Maybe. Why?" Never make it easy for a guy. It's the Allie strategy.

"Want to go to a party?"

"With you?"

Tad made a loud crash when he threw the hose against the building.

"Yeah. Any interest?" Rand asked.

Amazing. He was asking me out when I was sopping wet with limp hair and no makeup. Probably because my shirt was clinging to my body and because he remembered what I looked like when I cleaned up. He certainly wouldn't be interested if I was just a soppy, makeupless girl. "I'll have to check my schedule. I'll let you know tomorrow."

"Allie, we have to get to work. Are you ready?" Tad shoved my gloves into my hand.

Great. The hostility was back in Tad's voice. I shot Rand an apologetic glance and left him standing there. Not that I was sorry about that. It was good to keep Rand on a string, even if it did mean I was once again alone with Tad.

I fell in beside Tad, my feet making these loud squishing noises with each step. He said nothing, and neither did I.

I couldn't think of a single thing to say. Since when did I get tongue-tied around boys? I never cared what I said. If they liked me, great. If they didn't, who needed them? Plenty of others around.

So why was Tad different?

It couldn't be the bet. I wasn't even going to participate in it.

He stopped in the middle of another field. "Carrots again."

Carrots. I hated carrots. Not that it mattered. I dropped to my knees and began digging.

Tad didn't move to the next row. Instead, he worked beside me. We filled crate after crate together. After a while, he cleared his throat. "Are you mad about the hose?"

I eyed him. Was he hoping I'd be mad? Would that be a sign that he'd successfully messed with me? Or was he feeling bad? He was concentrating on the carrots, though, so I couldn't see his face. Forced to answer without knowing his motivation, I decided to go with the truth. "I'm not mad. I thought it was kind of funny actually. At least it was when you guys got wet. Rand looked so mad, it was hilarious."

He manhandled a bunch of carrots out of the dirt. "You like Rand?"

I shrugged. "I don't know. You like Natalie?"

He looked up quickly. "You mean, *like* her?"

"Uh-huh."

"Is that what she thinks?"

"No. She thinks you're just friends. I think you like her." Discussing his liking of Natalie wasn't top on my list of conversation topics, but at least he was communicating with me. It was a start.

He glanced at me. "She's nice. Fun."

"I can be fun." I yanked at a carrot and threw it in the crate. And I did notice that he didn't confirm or deny whether he *liked* her.

After a few more minutes of silence, I sat back on my heels and rested my muddy gloves on my thighs. These jeans were so toast. "Can I ask you something?"

He didn't look up. "Sure."

"Why don't you like me?" At his sharp look, I added, "Not like as in *like* like, just like."

He was quiet for so long I thought he wasn't going to answer. But finally he said, "I'm here to work. When I saw you the first day, you looked like you'd be afraid of hard work and avoid it. I figured you'd slow me down and complain all day."

"And now?"

He grinned. "You do slow me down."

"And the complaining?"

"Not as bad as I thought."

73

I nodded and felt better. Not sure why. But I did. Didn't even feel the same level of antipathy toward carrots.

My friends and I went to my house for pizza after work. Blue's mom had offered to cook us dinner but we were too hungry to survive on her food. The organic vegetarian stuff was hard to take sometimes. Plus Colin and Theo liked to hang out at my house where there were no parents around. It cramped their style to be hanging around Blue's parents, especially Theo, who was Blue's brother.

We hadn't even started eating when Natalie brought up that sordid topic. "So, what are the terms of the wager? You can't keep avoiding the topic forever, Allie."

Colin looked interested. "What's the wager?"

"Natalie . . ."

"There's this guy at work named Tad who doesn't like Allie. Blue and Frances said you two claimed there are guys who are immune to her charms, and they think Tad is one of them. I disagree. So we have a wager about whether she'll win him over by the end of the summer."

I shoved a piece of cheese pizza in my mouth and ignored everyone.

"So, is it true?" Natalie continued. "You two don't have the hots for Allie?"

Theo rolled his eyes. "What are you trying to do, get us in trouble? Either we insult our girlfriends' best friend or we say we like someone other than our girlfriends? No way."

Colin nodded his agreement. "Dangerous topic. I'm staying out of it." He shot Blue a look that suggested he wasn't too high on the subject, which made me think that he really had said that about me in the first place and didn't want me to know.

Not that I was interested in Colin, but had he really told Blue that there was nothing appealing about me? Nothing too warm and fuzzy about that.

The pizza suddenly tasted like cardboard, and I set it down.

"So, what's the wager?" Natalie repeated. "We need some high stakes."

Blue grinned. "The losers have to stuff their bras on the first day of school for the whole day."

I couldn't help but laugh, but Natalie looked horrified. "No way."

Yeah, I guess the stakes would be higher at a coed school. Still, it would be hysterical.

"Afraid you'll lose?" Blue said.

Natalie sat up. "Of course not."

Frances squirmed in her chair. "I'm not so sure about this stuffed bra thing. Can't we do something less public?"

"Plus, Allie's laughing. If she doesn't care, then she's not going to be inspired to win," Natalie said.

"Give me a break. The glory of getting the guy will be enough for her," Blue said.

"Oh, really?" I sat up. "Have you ever seen me go after a guy after he's shown no interest? Ever? Have I ever spent one minute on a guy who didn't return the interest?"

"You don't spend more than one minute even on guys who do return the interest," Frances said.

She had a point.

"Besides, I'm not going after Tad. Rand already asked me to a party this weekend."

Theo held up his hand. "Wait a sec. Rand and Tad? Their last name wouldn't be Novak, would it?"

Something clunked in my gut, and I looked at Theo. "The owner of the farm stand is named Mr. Novak. Sam Novak. But I don't know Tad and Rand's last names." I looked at my friends, who all shrugged.

"It's gotta be the same ones," Theo muttered.

"Same who?" Theo went to the public school in town, so he knew lots of guys that I didn't, courtesy of my miserable existence at an all-girl's school.

"The Novaks. There's a Rand Novak who plays lacrosse for Medfield. And I think his younger brother is a runner. Tad, right?" Theo rubbed his chin. "Rand's really good. Can't stand the guy. Got in my way every time we played them."

Brothers?

"What about Sam Novak?" Frances asked. "Do you know him?"

Theo looked thoughtful. "I think he might be Rand's brother too. There are a bunch of kids in that family, spread out a lot. Could be an uncle or something, I guess. How old is he?"

"He graduated from college three years ago," I said. I'd made a point of finding out about Mr. Novak when he showed up on the first day of Latin class. He was hot and young and I needed the scoop.

"Could be a brother, then. I think Tad's the youngest."

No way.

Natalie looked thrilled. "Well, given that Rand has the hots for Allie and Mr. Novak wants to fire both of us, it certainly makes things even more interesting if they're all related. Throw in some brotherly competition, and who knows what will happen? I say this bet is on, only we'll make it that the losers have to stuff their bras at the first school dance of the year. That way everyone has to do it around boys."

There was a general murmur of assent for the terms, but I was too busy digesting the new information.

Rand, Tad and Mr. Novak. All brothers.

I wasn't sure where that left me.

Not sure at all.

Chapter Five

We'd been cutting flowers for three hours before I drummed up the nerve to ask Tad. He'd been halfway decent all morning, but he'd rolled his eyes at my tube top. Why couldn't he appreciate my fashion sense?

I refused to dress like a dirt heap just to impress him. I liked looking good. In fact, it was the only thing I could do to try to make people like me, so if I stopped taking care with my appearance, then what? I'd just be another loser with parents who didn't care and no boyfriend or talents whatsoever.

So I painted my nails to match my shirt, curled my hair, put on my makeup and went to work cutting flowers. Until I couldn't stand it anymore. "Are you and Rand brothers?"

His shoulders tensed and he nodded.

I waited for him to say something, but he didn't.

"Is Sam your brother too?"

Another nod.

"So, you're the youngest?"

He looked at me. "Why do you care?"

Yeesh. Nice hostility. Someone had a little baggage about his family. "Just making conversation."

"Fine." He dropped a handful of flowers in the bucket. "You ready to take this back?"

"Sure." I didn't know what I'd said to make him mad, but the tense truce of the morning was definitely gone.

I followed him across the field with my trusty wheelbarrow. I'd tied red ribbons on the handles to make it cheerier, seeing as how I got the same one every day. I wasn't going to be afraid to admit I liked pretty things no matter how much it pissed Tad off.

We reached a shed behind the main farm stand. Natalie, Blue and Frances were in there arranging flowers, and Rand was moving boxes.

"We have more flowers," Tad announced.

Rand was by my side in an instant, taking my wheelbarrow and pushing it the rest of the way. "How are you doing, Allie?"

I grinned. "Great."

"You look cute."

WHO NEEDS BOYS?

Tad dropped his wheelbarrow with a loud thud. "So, Natalie, want to go camping this weekend?"

I spun around to see Natalie's eyes widen in surprise, and then they narrowed in thought.

"Camping with whom?" She made a pretense of picking extra leaves off the flower she was working on, but she wasn't fooling me. She was totally concentrating on Tad, and I could see she was trying to form a plan.

Well, she could forget it if that plan included me. I'd stuff my bra in public long before I'd crawl along after someone who didn't want me.

"My family," Tad said. "We're going up to Maine. My parents, a couple of my sisters and maybe some other people. I'm never sure exactly who is going to show up. Probably at least ten people, though."

She rubbed the back of her hand across her forehead. "I don't know. I've never gone camping before."

"It'll be fun." Tad glanced at me. "No running water, though."

I almost stuck my tongue out at him. Like I couldn't survive without running water.

"Well, I'll go if Allie goes," Natalie said.

Yikes! What was that?

Tad shot me a scowl, and I glared back. "I didn't tell her to say that," I said, lest he think I was angling to get him.

"Hey, that's a good idea." Rand's hand settled on my shoulder and turned me toward him. "I'll go too."

Now, that certainly changed things. "What about your party?"

He shrugged. "This will be more fun. Maybe we can go swimming. Make sure you bring your bikini."

Tad snorted and I felt my cheeks heat up. Rand was certainly making his thoughts about me clear. It was a little embarrassing in front of everyone else.

"Great. It's a deal." Natalie nodded at Tad. "Allie and I will go."

"Sweet." Rand gave me a private little smile that made my pedicure curl. "You been camping before?"

"No." I didn't even glance at Tad, because I knew he'd be shooting me some disdainful look implying how pathetic I was for not being an outdoor nature girl.

"Don't worry. We're all experts." He nodded at Tad. "We have enough extra supplies for them, don't we? They don't need to bring anything?"

Tad shrugged. "I guess."

What was his problem?

Rand touched my arm. "All you need to pack is your personal supplies. Bring warm clothes and rain gear in case it's raining. And stuff for hot days in case we get good weather. We'll leave from work on Friday, so have your bag with you."

I looked at Natalie. We were really doing this? Going off for the weekend with Rand and Tad? Granted, their parents were going to be there, but camping? Like in the woods? With no running water?

I mean, Rand was cute and everything, but come on! Wasn't this going a little too far outside my comfort zone for a guy? Totally against my rules. I mean, wouldn't my mom freak about me going off camping with a bunch of people I didn't even know?

No, she wouldn't. Neither would Dad. I could do whatever I wanted.

Great.

"So, you on?" Rand's hand was still on my arm, and he was looking at me. Isn't that sweet? He wasn't taking Natalie's word as mine.

I managed a smile. "Sure. I'll go."

Rand nodded and flashed me a bone-melting grin. "Good."

Tad sort of grimaced. "Great." Almost as an afterthought, he looked at Blue and Frances, who were nearly drooling with excitement over the discussion. "You guys want to come too? I'm sure we have enough tents."

Frances immediately shook her head. "We have boyfriend obligations this weekend. But thanks for the offer."

Blue nodded her agreement. "I'm not really the camping type. But you guys have fun. We'll look forward to a report."

Yeah, I'm sure they would. They'd be snuggled with their boyfriends on a couch watching television while I was fighting off rabid bears trying to kill me.

And to think, before my dad canceled on me, I'd been bummed that I'd miss out on summer in Boston with my friends. Even severe sunburn and a vomiting pregnant woman would have been better than this.

"You want to back out?" Tad was studying me, and there was a hint of hope in his eyes.

Fat chance of that. As if I'd ever admit to Tad I was worried about roughing it in the woods. I could handle sleeping in the great outdoors—as long as there were no bears!—and I was going to prove it. "No."

He eyed me, and I eyed him back. "Fine."

"Fine."

Rand set his hand on Tad's shoulder. "Hey, little brother, chill out. I'll keep her occupied so she doesn't cramp your style."

Tad shrugged Rand's hand off, grabbed his wheelbarrow and left, pausing in the doorway to bark at me. "Coming?"

"Wouldn't miss out on a chance to spend more quality time with you." My sarcasm was lost on Tad, though, as he was already long gone. I glowered at the door briefly before turning to smile sweetly at Rand. Then I picked up my wheelbarrow and went to find Tad.

Yes, I was really looking forward to this weekend. Not. How did I get myself into these situations?

My mom came into my room Thursday night when I was packing. Her highlighted hair was perfectly curled to accent her cheekbones, and she had on a cute little workout outfit. Black stretch pants, a sports bra and new Nikes. On someone my age, it would be a hot outfit. But she looked like someone trying to be twenty years younger than she was. All the better to attract men with, right? "Hi, Allie."

It was the first time I'd seen her in three days. "What are you doing home?"

"Jack had plans with his daughter tonight."

"Who's Jack?" I picked up a pair of ugly gray wool socks. Fashion or comfort? I decided to throw them in the duffel bag. I didn't have to show them to anyone, but I didn't want to freeze to death up there. Maine. The woods. At night. In a tent.

How awful did that sound?

My mom sat on my bed, right on top of my cute tops. "He's the man I've been seeing."

"Only one? What happened to all the others?" I tugged my clothes out from under her butt and set them in the duffel. Three short-sleeved shirts. Was that enough? Maybe more. What if I got dirty?

She handed me my jeans. "There's been only one for a while. I think you should meet him."

"No, thanks." As if I needed that in my life.

"He wants us all to go to dinner on Friday night. He'll bring his daughter and then you and I will join them."

My stomach instantly congealed into a lump. So that's where my mom had been lately? Hanging out with Jack and his daughter? Instead of her own daughter, she was being a mom to someone else's kid? I kept my voice level as I tucked a couple of sweatshirts in the bag. "You know his daughter well?"

"Oh, yes. She's darling. You'll love her. She's going into tenth grade like you. She's a very talented athlete. In fact, she plays varsity softball."

I put a pair of boots in my bag. "You've gone to watch her play?"

"Several times." My mom handed me my bathing suit, lifting her eyebrow at the skimpy nature of it. "You wear this in public?"

"Yep." I snatched it from her and shoved it into my bag. "How else am I going to get boys to look at my breasts?"

The shock factor worked, and my mom looked startled. "Is that what your goal is? To have boys look at your breasts?"

"Yep." I shoved a couple of bras into my bag, then retrieved a beach towel from under my sink. "Isn't that what you taught me? Live for boys gawking at my body? I mean, what else is there in life besides divorcing your husband and then hooking up with as many men as possible?"

"Allie!" my mom snapped. "Enough of that."

I slammed the towel into my bag. "Forget it. You've lost the right to be my mother. Dropping into my room once a week to tell me not to talk about breasts doesn't satisfy the minimum requirements of being a mom."

"Allie Morrison, you will not talk to me that way." She was on her feet now, and her cheeks were red.

Tough. "I can't go meet Jack and his precious daughter because I'm going away this weekend. Camping."

"Where? With whom?"

"If you were a part of my life, you'd know the answer to that." I zipped up my bag. "Ask Natalie's mom. She's met them." Natalie's mom had made a point of introducing herself to Mr. Novak, Tad and Rand on her carpool day this week. Apparently, Mr. Novak had satisfied her, because she'd given Natalie permission to go. After, of course, she'd talked to their mom on the phone.

"Natalie's mom? What does she know?"

"A lot more than you." I slung my bag over my shoulder. "I'm going to sleep at Blue's tonight." I hadn't planned to sleep over at Blue's, but I wasn't in the mood to be home. Besides, if I stuck around, my mom might decide to play mom and try to ban me from going camping.

As much as I didn't want to hang around wild animals and dirt and a boy who didn't like me, it was suddenly looking extremely appealing. Let's see. Go camping or go to dinner with my mom and her new boyfriend and his wonderful daughter who had won over my mom's heart?

Gee. Such a tough decision.

"Allie, you aren't going out tonight. You're going to stay here and talk to me."

I looked at her. Did she really care? Did she actually want me around?

Or was it an ego thing? Did she not want to have to admit to Jack that she had no relationship with her own daughter anymore?

"Why do you want me to stay?"

She frowned. "Because you can't walk out on me like this."

So it was the ego.

Stupid of me to think it might be because she actually wanted me around.

"If you go out tonight, I won't let you go camping."

I let my bag drop to the floor. "Really?" How could she stop me? It would require her to stay home and keep an eye on me, and we both knew that wasn't going to happen.

My mom hesitated. "Stay here tonight, Allie. Catch me up on your life."

"You're my mom. You're supposed to be caught up."

"That's what I want. Stay and talk."

"Do you have any idea how upset I was when Dad cancelled on me? I needed you, and you were off with someone else's kid instead of your own."

"Oh, Allie. I'm so sorry. Why didn't you say anything?"

"How could I? I never see you." I picked up my bag again and blinked back my stupid tears. "I'm going over to Blue's house. I'm leaving straight from work, so I'll see you Sunday night. If you're around."

I wanted her to stop me when I walked out. I wanted her to grab me by the arm and order me to my room. To shout that she loved me and she was my mother and nothing was going to change that.

But she didn't.

She let me go.

Probably figured she could go see Jack and his stupid daughter since I wasn't going to be around.

When I got to Blue's house, she was out on a date with Colin, and Theo was out with Frances.

So I played Xbox with her nine-year-old sister Marissa, ate disgusting health food with her parents for dinner, and then went to bed in their guest room.

Great night. If Tad could see me now, he'd really think I was pathetic.

Rand threw my bags in the back of his pickup, along with his bags, Tad's bags, Natalie's bags and a bunch of camping equipment. And despite the thought of bugs creeping into my sleeping bag and bats dive-bombing my head at night, I was excited.

Who cared if Tad didn't like me? Rand did, and that was enough.

"Shotgun," Natalie yelled, elbowing me out of the way as she dove into the front seat. Seeing as how Rand was the only one with a driver's license, that meant that Tad and I would be in the backseat together.

Except Rand caught her arm. "Why don't you sit in back with Tad?"

Yes, that's right. I didn't want to be snuggled down with an Allie-hater.

Natalie fluttered her eyelashes. "I get carsick in the backseat. Trust me, you don't want me riding back there."

Total liar. She didn't get carsick. "Natalie. Get in the back."

She glared at me. "You want me to lose, don't you?"

"No, I just don't care about the stupid bet." And I wasn't about to sit in the back of the truck with Tad for four hours. Rand was my man, and I was giving him my full attention.

"What bet?" Rand asked.

"Yeah, what bet?" Tad echoed.

Um . . .

"I'll get in back." Natalie pulled open the back-door of the extended cab and slipped into the small backseat of the pickup. "Come on, Tad."

Tad flashed me a look, but he climbed in.

Good. Let them be all cozy. I wasn't interested in some up close and personal time with Tad. In fact, I wasn't all that interested in close and cozy with any-one. I liked my space, which is why I was boyfriend-less. My choice, not because of a lack of suitors.

Rand would be good for a fling and a keep-it-casual ego boost, which is what I needed.

Mr. Hot opened my door for me and held out his hand. "Your chariot awaits."

Total hunk. I put my hand in his and let him assist me into the truck. After all, once we'd finished working I'd changed into a fun little skirt that didn't work too well for climbing into pickup trucks.

He settled me, and then tucked my legs in. "You look cute."

I grinned. "Thanks."

"She looks like she's going to a party, not camping," Tad said.

My good feeling immediately faded and I threw a glare back at him. "Why can't you be nice?"

He looked surprised. "I'm nice."

"How is that nice?"

Rand shut my door and walked around the front of the truck.

"I just said you looked like you were going to a party. I wasn't disagreeing that you looked cute."

"So you think I look cute?"

Tad opened his mouth to respond, then Rand pulled open the driver's door and got in. "Everyone all set?"

Tad shut his mouth and leaned back in the seat. What had he been about to say? Would he have admitted he thought I was cute? Or would it have been some other insult?

And why did I care anyway?

I pondered that thought for the first hour of the ride. Well, I pondered it for part of the hour. The rest of the time I was listening to Tad and Natalie whisper in the back and feeling very very lonely.

Chapter Six

"Anyone want to play a game?" Natalie spoke loud enough that it was apparent that those of us in the front seat were invited to respond. About time she remembered she was there with me. Wasn't she supposed to be working on Tad for me? What if she decided she liked him? Since he obviously liked her, it didn't take a rocket scientist to figure out that they'd become a couple.

That would leave me as the only one of the four of us without a boyfriend.

Which was how I wanted it. I didn't want a boyfriend. Why would I want to get tangled up with any one guy? It gave them too much power over me. My dad had made it quite evident that it was no good to depend too heavily on one guy.

Independence and no commitment was the only way to go.

Which was why Rand was perfect for me. He had the aura of a player, yet he still thought I was cute. Casual but fun. Exactly what I wanted.

"Sure, we'll play," Rand said.

We will? I wasn't so sure about that.

"Allie and I will be a team," Rand added.

We will? I didn't hear myself agree to that one.

"You want to partner up?" Tad asked Natalie. See? That was how it was supposed to be. Consultation before a decision was made. None of this making decisions for me.

Natalie agreed despite me sending her mental vibes to the contrary.

I turned around in my seat, annoyed to see that Natalie and Tad were actually touching shoulders. Granted, they had no choice because the seat was already small, plus there were camping supplies on the seat next to Tad, but still.

It almost made me wish I'd let Natalie feign the carsickness. "What are we playing?"

"Outburst. I brought it for the ride." Natalie handed me a scorecard. "Everyone know how to play?"

"We don't." Rand again. What, were he and I the same person or something? Or maybe he'd decided I'd lost the ability to speak and think on my own. Either way, it was getting a little irritating.

"Actually, I know how." I turned to Rand. "Each card has a topic, and then we have to guess what ten items are listed under that topic. Like, the topic might be 'colors' and then we'd list all the colors we could think of and hope we get all ten. And then we roll dice for bonus points. Plus you get three passes. If you pass, you have to do the next card no matter what, and the other team gets the one we passed on. Got it?"

He nodded. "Are you smart? I don't like to lose."

What kind of question was that? "I'm not an idiot." I wasn't a brainiac like Frances and I didn't study that much, but I wasn't a dumb blonde either.

I noticed Tad didn't ask Natalie if she was smart.

Using the lid of the cooler to keep the dice from flying around, we rolled to see who went first, and the backseat won. So I pulled a card out of the stack and read the title. "Dog breeds."

Natalie and Tad immediately ducked heads and whispered frantically, no doubt trying to see how many types they knew. I wished it didn't bug me that they made such a good little team. After a moment, Tad nodded. "We'll take it."

"Right." I slid the card into the reader so I could see the answers. "Go."

They managed to name eight of the breeds and

got two bonus points from the dice. Good start. Jerks.

Natalie and Tad gave each other a high five, then Tad pulled a card out of the stack. "Sandra Bullock movies."

"Chick flicks. We'll pass," Rand said.

"Hey!" I glared at Rand. "I know those."

Natalie grinned. "Too late. You already passed." She handed it to me to hold, then grinned at Tad. "I know all those."

He smiled back. "You're obviously the secret weapon on our team." Tad pulled out the next card. "Ancient Roman leaders."

"Oh, great." I folded my arms across my chest. "I suppose you know all these?"

Rand shot me a look. "No, I don't."

"Well, if you'd taken one second to consult me as your partner, then we could have gotten some points. I know way more Sandra Bullock movies than Roman leaders." Gee, this was fun. Natalie was getting all warm and cozy with Tad, who was being way nice, and I was stuck with Rand, who had some complex about being the macho man in charge of everything.

The game didn't improve. Rand continued to play as if he were the only one on our team, while Natalie and Tad worked together, pooling their knowledge. They killed us, and they had a great time.

Me, on the other hand? I almost wished I was at dinner with my mom, her new boyfriend and his daughter.

Well, maybe that was going a little too far, but I'd definitely rather be digging up carrots than watching a guy who didn't like me be so nice to my friend while his brother treated me like poop. Why wouldn't Tad treat me like he treated Natalie? He was nice. Sure, he was my age and therefore I wasn't interested in him, but everyone could use a friend, right?

But I had plenty of friends, and I certainly didn't need him.

By the time we reached the campsite, I was crabby and tired of Rand checking out my legs at every stoplight.

Natalie and Tad had gone to sleep in the backseat, using each other as pillows.

So cute.

I had a feeling that if I went to sleep I'd wake up with Rand's hand on my thigh. And for some reason, I wasn't in the mood for that, so I stayed awake and listened to Rand talk about himself and his lacrosse successes.

By the time we reached the campsite, it was almost eight o'clock. Three other cars were already there, and a bunch of tents were set up. There had to have been at least ten people hanging around playing Frisbee, plus some kids and two dogs. When Rand put the truck into park, I stared at the crowd. "Are you related to all these people?"

"Yep. Big family."

"I guess." It was so different from my family. I wasn't sure I was ready for some huge family event.

Then Rand opened my door and held out his hand to help me down. Guess I didn't have a choice, huh?

I could totally do this. "Give me a sec." I checked my makeup in his rearview mirror, fixed my hair and touched up my lip gloss. By the time I finished, Natalie and Tad were already in the middle of the group, and Rand was pulling bags out of the back.

Was I supposed to hop down and force my way into the group? There were no other kids our age for me to gravitate to. Just a bunch of adults and some really small kids. If there had been boys, I would have known how to deal with that. But adults?

Not so much.

So I avoided all of them and went to help Rand

unload. He shot me an appreciative smile. "Looking good, Allie."

"Thanks." I accepted two sleeping bags and tried not to watch Tad and Natalie laughing.

"Let's set up over here. Tad and I'll put our tent next to you and Natalie." He dropped his load next to the woods at the edge of the clearing, a little bit away from the other tents. "Look good?"

"I guess." I eyed the woods. Were there bears in these parts? Was having the tent so close to the forest a good idea?

Natalie flung her arm around my shoulders, her face flushed and her eyes dancing. "Is this fun or what?"

"Yeah. Fun."

Rand dropped a tent bag in front of us. "Have at it."

"Have at it?" Natalie frowned at the bag, and I knew she had no more idea than I did how to put it up.

"Everyone carries their own weight when we go camping." Rand tossed his tent about fifteen feet to the right. "Tad! Come set up!"

Tad moseyed over and gave me a once-over that made me want to tear off my skirt and throw on sweatpants. "What's up?"

Natalie answered. "We're putting up the tents, apparently."

I almost laughed at the dubious look on her face as she stared at the package on the ground. "Maybe you and I should just sleep under the stars. We can probably figure out how to unroll a sleeping bag."

She nodded slowly, then shook her head. "No, I want to learn. Let's have a contest."

I raised my eyebrow. "I think the guys might win, given that neither of us has any idea about how to put up a tent."

"No, we'll pair up with the guys." She looked mighty smug all of a sudden. "Since you and Rand are no match for Tad and me, we'll split up. You and Tad can team up, and I'll work with Rand."

Yeah, good luck. As if Rand would let her touch the tent. Which gave me an idea . . . "How about the first one with the tent up wins? And the boys can't touch the tents. They have to tell us what to do." Not that I really wanted to put the tent up myself, but I thought it would be hysterical to take power away from Rand. I knew it would bug him, and for some reason, I was in the mood to annoy him.

Couldn't be because he'd refused to let me even

open my mouth during the entire Outburst fiasco, could it? Nah.

Natalie frowned. "I don't know about that. Don't you have to pound stakes and stuff?"

"You can do it, Natalie." Tad said. "Rand's a good teacher."

I nearly fell over. Did that mean Tad wasn't going to object to being paired with me?

"I think Allie and I should try to redeem ourselves," Rand said. "We'll win this time."

I looked at Rand, standing there looking all hot in his shorts and T-shirt, and I really didn't want to try to work with him. He winked at me, and I wanted to throw the sleeping bag at his head.

Natalie glanced at me, and I tried to flick my eyes toward Rand and then give her the "I'm going to vomit" grimace.

She grinned, and marched over to Rand. "Sorry, Rand, but I think Allie wants a chance to win this time, and as her friend, it's my duty to give her that opportunity."

Rand eyed her. "You think Tad's better than me?"

"Isn't he?"

Next to me, Tad grinned. "You tell him, Nat."

Nat? So they were on a nickname basis already? So adorable.

Rand didn't look so amused. "My little brother can't beat me."

Tad's grin faded, and his jaw tightened. Guess he didn't like the little brother tag. I wouldn't either.

"Then you'll have to prove it, won't you?" Natalie flipped a glance over her shoulder at Tad and me. "Ready?"

I nodded. "I guess."

"Go!" She grabbed Rand's hand and dragged him over to their tent. He immediately bent over and grabbed for the bag. Natalie slapped his hand and Tad shouted, "For every infraction of the rules, add three minutes to your time."

Rand glared at us, and shoved his hands in his pockets. "Don't worry, little brother. I'll still crush you."

Tad shot him a look that wasn't all about brotherly love, then turned to the bag on the ground. He squatted down, grabbed my wrist and gently pulled me down next to him. "Okay, Allie, are you ready?"

"Sure."

He glanced over his shoulder, then lowered his voice. "Listen, I know you have the hots for Rand, but losing to him won't make him like you more. The best way to get him is to make him lose. Nothing gets his interest more than a challenge."

I tilted my head. "Are you sure you're not just telling me that because you don't want to lose?"

He grinned. "Whatever gave you the idea I didn't want to lose?"

"Oh, maybe the look on your face when he called you 'little brother'?"

His smile faded. "He's just trying to embarrass me in front of you and Natalie."

"Don't let him get to you."

He lifted a brow.

"Well, so what if you're his little brother? Plenty of hot guys are someone's little brother." I bit my lip. Did I really say that? Imply that Tad was a hot guy?

His smile returned. "You're not half-bad, Allie Morrison."

I smiled and got a warm feeling in my belly. "Back at you."

He nodded at the bag. "When you're ready."

I heard Rand curse at Natalie and I smiled more broadly. I was definitely going to owe Natalie after this one.

But first, I was going to win this contest for the little brother.

Ten minutes later, after we'd caught Rand for the third time with his hands on tent parts, Tad called for a referee. His dad and another brother came over to watch over each team, but within about five minutes, the rest of the family had decided we were the entertainment for the night.

Nothing like watching two bumbling city girls trying to put up tents under pressure to generate some serious entertainment for everyone else.

Tad and Rand's mom set up some lawn chairs and poured lemonade for the kids and handed out beer to the adults.

I leaned in next to Tad for a confidential whisper. "I can't do this with everyone watching."

"Sure you can." He pointed to a wooden thing. "That's a stake. We're going to need a hammer to pound it in."

I picked it up, and heard the kids chanting Natalie's name. "No, seriously, Tad. I have no idea what I'm doing." For a girl who preferred to project total confidence, competence and independence, being on center stage as a bumbling fool wasn't exactly high on my list.

Tad must have realized I was serious, because he put his arm around me and walked me away from the group for a second. "Allie."

"What?"

He turned me toward him and put his hands on

my shoulders. "First of all, you might not know about tents, but I do, right?"

I'd never realized how long and dark his eyelashes were. "Yeah."

"And Natalie knows no more than you, right?"

"Yes, but . . ."

"And we know Rand's not going to be able to keep his hands off the tent parts, so they'll be incurring penalties constantly."

I giggled. "That's true. Rand's kind of a control freak."

Something flickered in his eyes. "You noticed?"

"Of course I did. I was on his team for Outburst. How could I not notice?"

"And it bugs you?"

I frowned. "Of course. Why?"

He shook his head. "No reason. But listen to me, you're perfectly capable of putting up a tent. We'll work together and it'll be fine."

"But I'll look like a dork."

"Who cares? It's all about fun. We're not up in the woods of Maine for a beauty contest."

Was that another slam on me because I liked to look good?

Tad rolled his eyes. "Give me a break, Allie. You look great, so stop worrying about it. Just have fun.

That's what it's about." He grinned. "And it's about beating up on my brother."

I grinned back. "Does he get cranky when he loses?"

"Absolutely."

Then I realized that he'd just said I looked great. He'd noticed? He didn't think I looked stupid?

"Allie?"

I blinked. "What?"

"You ready to have fun and not worry about what anyone else thinks? It's just you and me out there. Okay?"

Me and him? A team? Having fun?

A smile crept across my face. "Okay."

He grinned. "Okay."

Then he slung his arm around my shoulder and walked me back toward the pile of poles and blue nylon on the ground.

"You guys lost precious time," his mom said. She was in the lawn chair closest to us.

"Strategy discussion," Tad said. "It's always important to have a plan."

I grinned. He could have said his partner had had a complete breakdown and needed a pep talk, but he hadn't. He'd stuck with me.

Rand shouted something at Natalie, and Tad

nudged me with his shoulder. "So, Ms. Morrison, how about we build this sucker?"

The crowd started chanting my name, and I grinned. "Let's do it."

Chapter Seven

"We're done!" Tad grabbed my hand and held it over my head. "Allie wins!"

I grinned as the crowd cheered, and laughed as Rand threw down a hammer and glared at us. Natalie was grinning and clapping, and Tad looked very pleased.

And I felt great. Great! I grinned at Tad. "It's because you're such a great teacher."

He shrugged, but his eyes were still glowing. "I managed not to incur any penalties. That's a good start."

Tad's mom stood up. "I think the losers have to clean up after dinner. Anyone disagree?"

Only Rand and Natalie protested, but they were vastly outnumbered by the swarm of Novaks.

A grill was unloaded from the back of one of the trucks and fired up. Hot dogs and hamburgers appeared, along with fruit salad, chips and corn on the cob. "How are you going to cook the corn?"

Rand grabbed the bag of corn. "We get it wet first. Come on." He took my hand and started walking away from camp with me.

Tad was talking to Natalie, but I saw him stop talking and watch us walk away. I couldn't read his face, but he wasn't grinning.

And suddenly I felt stupid walking off with Rand. I wanted to stay with everyone else. "Um, Rand, maybe I should stay and help."

"We'll be back in five minutes," he said. "Besides, I haven't had a minute alone with you yet."

Yeah, I'd noticed. And it hadn't bothered me a bit.

Then I frowned. What was wrong with me? I was on this camping trip to be with Rand, wasn't I? He was seventeen, hot and thought I was cute. What else did I want in a guy? Nothing. It was all about Rand. So I smiled at him. "Well, let's go, then."

He grinned back and led the way down a path to the edge of the lake. "We have to soak the corn so it doesn't catch fire on the grill. Then it gets grilled the way any burger would."

"Really?" I kicked off my sandals and waded into the water. "It's so warm." The water was so clear I could see every grain of sand on the bottom of the lake.

"Want to go swimming?"

"I don't have a suit on."

"So? Who needs a suit?"

Skinny-dipping? No way! "Rand!"

He shrugged and toed off his sneakers. "Why not? We do it all the time when we go camping."

Yeah, well, I wasn't in the mood to be stripping in front of him. "Sorry, but that's not going to happen."

He waded in after me and caught my hands. "Have I told you how cute you look in that outfit? It's the first time I've seen someone wear a skirt camping, but you carry it off." He trailed his hand over my thigh. "You have great legs."

I shoved his hand away. "Thanks."

He put his hand back on my thigh and cupped my chin with his other hand. "I've been wanting to kiss you all night."

This was what I wanted, wasn't it? I mean, I kissed guys all the time. Lots of guys. So what was my problem? Since when did I not want to kiss a guy? It made no sense at all. Rand was perfect for me. Cute, old and going away to school in the fall. Then I frowned. Or maybe he wasn't. I'd assumed he was Theo's age, but he could be going into his senior year. "Are you going away to college in the fall?"

He rubbed his thumb over my lower lip. "Let's not talk about the fall. We're here tonight; that's what matters."

That was a philosophy I generally subscribed to. Boys were for entertainment. Interchangeable objects that I could exchange and not notice the difference. No long-term baggage.

Rand was all of that.

So I was going to kiss him, like I kissed everyone else.

I put my hands on his chest and lifted my face to his. "I want to know whether you're going to college in the fall." No, I didn't! What was my problem? Who cared if he was leaving?

He tangled his fingers in my hair. "Allie, it doesn't matter where I'm going to be in the fall, does it? You know we'll both be with other people by then."

I frowned.

"Or am I wrong? I thought you were the type to have fun and move on?"

All of a sudden, I thought of my dad. Having fun and moving on. Leaving me behind without a second thought. It sucked, and I was tired of it. Not that I wanted a huge commitment, but today, the thought of having some guy walk away from me . . . I didn't want it.

So I pushed him away from me. "I'm not in the mood."

"Why not?" He tried to pull me back toward him, so I shoved him hard and caught my foot under his, dumping him on his butt in the water. "Allie!"

I ignored him and walked back to camp.

When I returned, Tad and Natalie were busy carving out a watermelon and they were laughing. Natalie had no makeup on, her T-shirt was stained with watermelon juice and her hair was shoved up in a crooked ponytail, and Tad was grinning at her like she was the best thing he'd ever seen.

I looked around. Everyone seemed to be busy getting dinner ready, or chatting with someone. It was family at its fairy-tale best, and I felt so out of it. My fault. I could be down at the lake with Rand getting cozy. I would have been in my comfort zone. But now?

I just wanted to go home.

"Allie!" Natalie waved at me. "Come help!"

Tad looked up sharply, then I saw him look past me, no doubt searching for Rand.

"No, I'll just take a nap." I wasn't in the mood to be a third wheel.

"Don't be ridiculous." Natalie grabbed my arm and pulled me over to the watermelon. "Sit down and help." She put a knife in my hand and a watermelon quarter on my lap, on my cute little skirt.

"Um, Nat?"

"What?" She sat down next to me and started carving again.

I looked at Tad, who was watching me out of the corner of his eye, and I decided not to complain about my skirt.

"So, where's Rand?" Tad asked.

I shrugged. "I left him at the lake."

"Why?"

"Because." I couldn't explain what I didn't really understand.

"Did he . . . um . . . do something to you?" There was an undercurrent of tension in Tad's voice that gave me goose bumps.

I looked up to find him staring at me intently, his knife immobile over the watermelon. Did he care? Was he worried about me? A warm feeling settled in my belly. "Nothing I couldn't handle."

Tad narrowed his eyes. "What does that mean?"

"It means I'm fine." It felt so weird to have someone worried about me. I should resent it, right? I mean, I don't need anyone.

But a little part of me wanted to roll over and bask in it. For a minute. That's all I wanted. One minute of someone caring what happened to me.

Tad's gaze left my face and flicked over my shoulder. Then his mouth curved up. "Rand's all wet."

"Is he?" I kept my voice as innocent as I could and plunged my knife into the watermelon. "I have no idea how that happened."

Tad looked at me again. "You're dry."

"Uh-huh."

"So, you didn't roll around in the water with him?"

I glared at him. "Of course not. What kind of question is that?"

"Just trying to put the pieces together." His voice was soft, but it was hard at the same time. "Did Rand deserve to get dunked?"

"Probably not."

"What does that mean?"

I flicked a watermelon seed at him. "It means I'm probably overly sensitive right now."

"Why?"

"Because I am." Talking about my dad with Tad would be too weird. It would make me sound like a whining loser.

Tad put his hand on my arm. "Allie."

I stared at his hand. "What?"

"What did Rand do to you that got him dunked?" There was tension in his voice again. "Tell me."

I swallowed and dragged my gaze off his hand, which was still on my arm. My eyes met Tad's. I had never realized what an interesting shade of green they were. "We discovered we had differing philosophies about certain things." I wasn't used to someone wanting to fight my battles for me, and I wasn't sure how I felt about it. "It's not a big deal, Tad. Let it go."

He looked like he wanted to say something else, but he pulled his lips together and shrugged. "If you want to talk, I'm around."

I swallowed and focused on my watermelon. What was up with the tears burning in my eyes? A little kindness from Tad and I was some ball of emotional mush? Ridiculous.

I cleared my throat and blinked several times. There would be no tears or any kind of dependent behavior from me. So what if I suddenly wanted nothing more than to spill all my miserable guts to Tad? Not going to happen.

"You guys almost finished with the watermelon?" Tad's mom hollered. "Burgers are done."

"Yep." Tad gathered up all the pieces that Natalie and I had sliced, then carried the platter over to the picnic table, but not before he gave me a small nod and a half smile.

I watched him walk away, and I felt so confused.

He was wearing his camping shorts again, with a pocketknife hanging off the waist and a water bottle on his left hip. Tad was not the kind of guy who would care what the kids at school were wearing or thinking. Not my kind of guy at all.

"He's cute, huh?" Natalie leaned on my shoulder and sighed. "Such a nice guy too."

"You two seem to be getting along."

"As friends, only."

"Maybe to you. He obviously likes you."

"He couldn't stop looking toward the lake once you and Rand headed down there."

I turned my head so I could see her face. "Really?"

"And look at him now. What do you suppose they're talking about?"

I followed her glance and saw Tad and Rand in a heated discussion at the edge of the woods. Tad was a good five inches shorter than Rand, but he was leaning forward and giving Rand some serious heat. Rand was giving it right back, and he looked big and tough.

And Tad wasn't backing down.

"You don't think they're talking about me, do you?" I was fascinated by the interaction. Was Tad really out there defending my honor against the big bully? It was the weirdest feeling, and not something I ever would have expected from Tad.

First of all, he didn't like me. Second of all, he hardly seemed like the type to take on Rand. He seemed more interested in pruning flowers and staking tomatoes than worrying about a girl he didn't even like.

Then I saw Rand look over at me, and Tad did the same.

Yikes. I immediately pretended to clean my knife. "Are they still looking over here?"

"No. Their dad is over there now trying to straighten it out," Natalie said.

I risked another glance. Their dad had his hands on the boys' shoulders, and was giving them a major lecture. Both Tad and Rand still looked mad and were glaring at each other. "Can you sneak through the woods and see if you can hear what's going on?"

Natalie snorted. "Yeah, that'll be me. City girl tromping through the woods to sneak up on a family squabble."

"You could at least try."

"Or you could ask Tad later on and find out from him."

"No way." As if! How egoistic would that be to ask him whether they were arguing about me? Besides, I didn't care. I didn't need boys and I certainly didn't need one to defend me.

WHO NEEDS BOYS?

* * *

We'd been in our sleeping bags for almost two hours, and I still couldn't go to sleep. "Nat?"

"What?"

"Are you awake?"

"No, I'm talking in my sleep."

I rolled over so I could face her, and kept my voice low. After all, Tad and Rand's tent was only a few feet away. "Can I ask you something?"

I heard her sleeping bag rustle and she sighed. "Yeah, sure. What?"

"If you hadn't made this bet about me and Tad, would you like him for yourself?" I didn't want to know, but at the same time, I had to know.

She moved around, then a flashlight snapped on and blinded me. "Sorry." She turned it to the side, so it lit up our faces but shone against the tent wall instead of in my eyes. "Allie, I swear I have no interest in Tad."

"But you guys seem to be so close."

Her cheeks were shadowed and pale in the beam of the flashlight. "He's my buddy. Like the guys on my track team. We're friends, we hang, we have fun. But that's all it is."

I studied her face, but her gaze didn't waver from mine. "Are you sure?"

"Absolutely. He doesn't do it for me."

"Why not?"

She rolled her eyes. "Oh, come on. There's nothing wrong with him. He just isn't the guy for me."

I digested that. "Have you told him that? Because I think he likes you."

"No, he likes you."

I turned the flashlight on her face, and she squinted. "How do you know? Did he say that?"

"He didn't have to." She batted the flashlight away. "It's obvious."

"How? Why?"

"Because it is."

I flopped on my back and stared at the tent ceiling.

"You like him?" Natalie asked.

"No."

"You like Rand?"

"Definitely not."

We were quiet for a minute, then Natalie said, "Do you think Tad is as much of a jerk as you originally thought?"

"No, but that doesn't mean I like him or anything."

"What's wrong with admitting you like a guy?"

"A lot." I could talk for hours about how wrong it was to admit you liked anyone. The instant you admitted that, even to yourself, you lost control of the situation. They could hurt you, like my dad had. I couldn't help how I felt about my dad, but I could make certain that no one else ever had that power. Which meant I didn't like any boy and I didn't care if they liked me.

Natalie didn't say anything, but it was almost dawn before I finally fell asleep.

When I woke up, the sleeping bag next to me was empty. Natalie's duffel was gone, and so was her pillow. My watch told me it was only eight o'clock. Natalie never got up that early. What was going on?

I stuck my head out of the tent, then promptly withdrew. Tad was in front of the tent talking to one of his other brothers—other than Rand, that is. I still hadn't gotten everyone's name down yet.

As I had told Natalie, I wasn't interested in Tad, but I certainly wasn't going to let him see me with bedhead, no makeup and wearing the T-shirt and sweats I'd slept in. So I retreated, found a hairbrush, put on some makeup and tried to look presentable.

FYI, it's a lost cause to look good after you've spent the night in a tent and have no bathroom available. Even my cute T-shirts were wrinkled, and something had spilled in my bag. Something that smelled like peaches and had spread a heavy oil stain on half my clothes.

Something that I identified as my Victoria's Secret body lotion after I dug my way through all my clothes and found the cap on one side of the bottom of my bag and the bottle on the other.

Bummer.

I salvaged one T-shirt, one pair of shorts, a pair of jeans, some underwear, my bathing suit, and that was it. So much for looking good for Tad. Or Rand. Or whoever. Myself. That's who I wanted to look good for. Myself.

Well, it wasn't going to happen. So I pulled on my only clean cute T-shirt, a pale pink cropped V-neck that showed off my stomach. Add my low-slung shorts and makeup to cover my oily skin (thanks to the lack of a shower), and I was halfway decent.

Except my hair. Yikes. Even the ponytail was lumpy. Almost bad enough to make me willing to wear a baseball cap.

Note to self: Camping is a *bad* idea if you want to impress a guy.

Finally, I gave up, threw the flaps aside and stepped out into the sun. Tad had moved off and was playing horseshoes with a couple of kids who were so small they could only throw the horseshoes about two feet. They looked really cute standing so close to the pegs and hurling the heavy horseshoes as hard as they could.

I glanced around, but saw no sign of either Rand or Natalie. The wonderful smell of bacon frying reached my nose though, and I decided I was glad I'd gotten up. Now, if only I could avoid seeing Rand or Tad until I got home tomorrow and had a chance to shower.

"Allie! Come over here!" Tad's mom gestured to me from the picnic table, where she was pouring glasses of orange juice. When I reached the table, she handed a glass to me. "Here you go."

I took a sip of the cold drink. It tasted awesome. "Do you have a fridge out here or something?"

She laughed and pointed to a truck with a bed cover on it. "We have a huge cooler in there. I have to confess, we like to camp with some of the comforts of home."

"When it comes to food at least." A woman whose name I couldn't remember, but who I thought was married to one of Tad's brothers, sat down next to me. "I'm Beth. Married to brother number four."

I nodded. "Thanks. I wish I was better at keeping everyone straight."

She indicated the two kids Tad was playing with. "They're mine. Thank heavens for Tad. It's nice to have a break." She filled her coffee cup and smiled at the horseshoe game. "He's so good with them."

I didn't turn around. I'd already noticed how well Tad interacted with the kids and I didn't want him to look up and see me watching him. "Are there any showers around?"

"Nope." Beth turned back toward me. "Take a jump in the lake. It's the best thing. Did you bring biodegradable soap?"

Was she kidding? "Um . . ."

"You can borrow mine." Tad's mom raised her voice. "Tad, go get some soap for Allie!"

"No, really, it's okay." I cringed when I glanced over my shoulder and saw Tad nod and head off toward the tents. "So, where's Natalie?" I didn't want to ask about Rand and give the impression I was looking for him.

"She left with Rand early this morning." Beth set a plate of bacon on the picnic table. "Grab some before the boys realize it's ready."

"What do you mean, she left?"

Tad's mom set a plate of scrambled eggs in front of me. Or rather, a massive platter of eggs and a stack of smaller plates and little forks. How weird was it to have a mom cooking breakfast for me? I kinda liked it, actually.

"Rand decided he didn't want to spend the weekend camping, and Natalie said she wanted to go as well. So they left."

"They left? As in, they aren't coming back?" How could she take off on me like that?

Tad's mom sat down across from me and put her hand over mine. "I'm sorry, Allie. I know you like Rand. Unfortunately, Rand's not a very good boyfriend. I hope you'll be able to have an okay time this weekend even if he's not here. We're really a fun group."

I stared at my Mom-for-the-Weekend. "Rand's gone?"

"Oh, dear, she's upset." Beth patted my shoulder. "Allie, I told them they should wake you up to see if you wanted to leave, but I was overruled."

I shook my head. "No, I don't care that Rand left." Well, I did care. I was psyched! "But why did Natalie leave?"

"Oh, I forgot." Tad's mom jumped up, grabbed a piece of paper from a canvas bag near the grill and handed it to me. "She left you a note."

A note. "Thanks."

I took it and turned away to read it.

Hey, Allie.

Have fun with Tad. I want all the details when you get home on Sunday.

Smooches,

Nat

I`folded the paper up and tried to catch my breath.

She'd left so I could be alone with Tad. Knowing Natalie, she'd probably convinced Rand to leave as well.

Tad and me.

Alone for the next twenty-four hours.

Alone except for the umpteen members of his family.

But alone, nonetheless.

Wow.

Chapter Eight

Tad shot me a wary look as he handed me the soap. "Morning."

"Hi." I tried to avert my face from him. Did I feel ugly or what?

"You going to wash your hair?"

"Why? Does it look bad?" I put my hands over my hair and cringed at the lumps, but Tad laughed.

"No, it looks fine. I just asked because Mom had me get you the soap."

"Oh, right." How could he think I looked fine? I looked horrible. But when I stole a glance at him, he smiled at me and sat down on the bench. He didn't cringe, or appear horrified by the Attack of the Ugly Girl. Simply smiled and helped himself to some eggs.

I wasn't quite sure what to do next.

Beth handed me a plate. "Eat."

Right. Eat. I could do that.

By the time I was halfway through my eggs, I felt like I was in the middle of a huge crowd. It was as if every member of the Novak clan had decided it was their duty to make me feel welcome after my friends had left.

And you know what? It worked. I wasn't lonely at all. I usually ate breakfast alone or skipped it altogether. This was way more fun, even when one of the little ones threw her orange juice all over me.

It gave me the motivation to get up from the table and go take my bath in the lake.

In my tent, I shed my stained clothes and pulled on my bikini. I threw my sleeping T-shirt over the top, wrapped my towel around my waist, slipped on my thongs and headed out.

Tad was waiting outside my tent in a bathing suit with a towel around his neck. "Hi."

My belly jumped a little. "Hey."

"Mom thought I should join you. You know, in case you started to drown or something. No one's allowed to go down to the lake alone."

It was weird to be around people who thought they needed to look out for me. It should cramp my style, but I kind of liked it. So I shrugged. "It's fine with me if you come down there."

He nodded and fell into step beside me.

We didn't talk until we were at the edge of the lake and I realized I was going to have to strip in front of him. I mean, I had my suit on, and I'd intentionally packed my bikini thinking that Rand was going to be there, but all of a sudden, I felt self-conscious. I mean, this was Tad, who had never been impressed with anything I'd worn or done to try to look good.

He dropped his towel and headed into the water, glancing back over his shoulder at me. "What's wrong?"

"Nothing." I could go swimming in my T-shirt, but it was my only clean shirt left, now that I had OJ on the one I'd worn this morning. Then again, Tad wouldn't notice me even if I went skinny-dipping, so why worry about wearing a bikini in front of him?

I bit my lower lip and dropped my towel and then pulled off my T-shirt. I glanced out at the lake, but Tad was underwater. I could see bubbles from him, but that was it.

I laughed at the feeling of disappointment that wafted through me when I realized Tad was giving me privacy. Was I psycho or what? *Make up your mind, Allie.*

Clutching my bottle of biodegradable soap, I waded out into the water until I was shoulder deep. At that point, Tad popped up beside me and flipped the water out of his face.

I wondered idly how clearly he'd been able to see me under the water, and if he'd even been looking.

Rand would have looked.

Not really Tad's style.

"Water feels great, huh?"

I nodded. "It's so warm."

"That's because it's shallow at this end of the lake. The other end, where it's a lot deeper, the water stays cold until August. That's why we like to camp on this side." He swam closer to me and I dropped the bottle of shampoo when I tried to open it.

No, it wasn't nerves because he was close to me. I'm a klutz. That's all.

Tad dove underwater and retrieved the bottle. He flipped the lid and handed it to me. "There you go."

"Thanks." Was I supposed to wash my hair with him in front of me? I'd never washed my hair in front of a guy before. It felt sort of weird. Intimate.

"Let me have some." He grabbed the bottle, poured a dollop into his hand, then rubbed it on his head to work up a lather. He grinned. "It won't make your hair turn green, I promise."

He looked so funny with a head full of suds that I laughed.

"Don't leave me hanging, Morrison." Tad took the bottle and squeezed some on my head. "Lather up."

"Hey!" I swatted his hand away, but it was too late. I could feel the cool liquid on my scalp. So much for not looking like a fool. Tad laughed as I dunked under the water, and then started scrubbing my hair. "Maybe I didn't want to wash it."

"Too late now." He grinned and dove under the water. I saw him beneath the surface rinsing the soap out of his hair.

How bizarre was this? Shampooing my hair in a lake with a guy.

Tad popped up. "You game for some hiking today?"

I continued to work the shampoo through my hair and tried not to wonder how bad I looked with suds dripping down my cheeks. No doubt, I was makeupless. Yet Tad didn't seem to be repulsed by my appearance.

Probably forgot to put in his contacts. "You wear contacts?"

"Nope." He flipped onto his side and began swimming in a circle around me. "Hike?"

"As long as it's not really hard. I've never been hiking before."

"We'll take it easy. Promise." He was behind me now, and I resisted the urge to turn around.

I washed my face with the biodegradable soap. It might not be my favorite facial scrub specially designed to decrease oil and prevent blackheads while still keeping skin soft and supple, but it was better than a face full of oil. "Then I guess I'll go."

"Good."

I dunked under the water and rinsed the soap off my face and out of my hair. When I came up, Tad was standing in front of me. He grinned when I came up. "Not bad for a first-time camper."

"What's not bad?"

"Washing in a lake. It takes some talent, you know."

I wasn't sure how to respond. He sounded sincere, but I wasn't used to anyone complimenting me on anything except my looks. Certainly not my shampooing skills.

"You might want to wear your bathing suit under your clothes when we go hiking."

"Why?" I wiped the water off my cheeks and realized he had nice eyes. Kind. And cute.

"Because the trail runs along the edge of the lake. When it gets hot, we hop in for a dip."

Somehow, the thought of swimming with Tad again didn't seem so bad. "Okay."

He nodded and began to float backwards toward shore. "You ready to head up?"

"I guess." I swam along beside him until the water was so shallow I had to stand up. When I did, Tad was already on the shore. I saw his eyes flick really briefly over my suit, then his cheeks went red and he turned away.

How cute was that? I mean, I still wanted a man and not a boy who would be embarrassed about those kinds of things, but it was still so cute. I mean, how could I not like that?

Tad draped his towel over his head and turned back to me, but the towel was over his face so he couldn't see anything. I burst out laughing. "Tad, it's just a bathing suit. You don't have to hide."

He pushed the towel to the side and looked at me out of one eye. "I'm not hiding."

"No?" I grabbed his towel and pulled it off. "Coulda fooled me."

He grabbed his towel back, but he slung it around his neck. "I'm not hiding."

"Good." I wrapped my towel around my shoulders and smiled to myself.

Tad was aware that I was a girl. Despite his best efforts to the contrary, he'd noticed.

And you know what? I was beginning to think that a boy wasn't such a bad thing.

Maybe.

Four hours later, I had gathered enough data to determine that I liked hiking. Or strolling, as Tad's brother Luke had kept complaining, albeit good-naturedly. He wanted the hardier members of the bunch to hop in the truck and drive twenty minutes to the mountains for a real climb, but Beth had insisted that he stay with them so he could carry the toddlers when they got tired. Which was pretty much all the time.

Tad had taken his turn with giving shoulder rides as well. He was pretty cute with them, actually. Hardly the egoistic older guy I usually liked, but he definitely had his appeal, especially now that he wasn't being mean to me.

I frowned. Why *was* he being nice? What had changed? Would he go back to the old Tad on Monday when we returned to Sam's Farm Stand?

Something bit my leg, and I slapped at my shin.

Then something else bit my knee, and I squawked and smacked my knee. A bee dropped to the ground. Then I got hit on my thigh, and then my shin again. "I'm being attacked!" I suddenly realized there were yellow and black buzzing things all around me! "Bee hive!"

Everyone started yelling and running, but no one was shrieking as loud as I was. "Help! Help!" Pain shot through my arm and I knew I'd been stung again. "Get them away from me!" I was screaming now and flailing my arms around my head where there were all sorts of murderous bees whizzing around. "Help!"

All of a sudden, Tad grabbed me from behind and nearly threw me into the lake.

"Hey!" I was crying now, everything hurt so much. "Stop it!"

"Get underwater!" He pulled me to my feet and dragged me deeper into the lake, then he grabbed my shoulders and pushed me under the water.

Once under, he nodded at me and pointed. He wanted me to swim, and I wanted to cry. He tugged on my hand and started swimming.

I had no choice but to follow, for about one second after which I needed air.

Tad followed me to the top, but as soon as my head broke the water, he said, "Take a breath and go back under. We need to swim far enough away from the bees."

As he said that, I heard more buzzing. Panic

seized me and I dove back under. This time Tad didn't have to tell me to swim. I swam as hard as I could. In fact, when I went under for the third time, Tad caught my arm and pulled me back up to the surface. "They're gone."

I tried to pull free. "No, we have to get farther away."

"Allie." He put one hand on my shoulder, using the other to tread water. "Look around. No bees."

I didn't want to look around, but I did. And I listened. All I heard was the shouting of his family on the shore and his breathing. Or was that mine? No, mine was the sniffling and crying. "You think they're gone?"

"Yes." He jerked his head toward the shore. "Let's head back."

"No!"

"We'll hit the shore farther up, away from them. Okay?" He raised his voice and shouted to his family. "Are there bees up there?"

"No," his dad shouted. "Come on over."

"See?"

Right. I took a deep breath and realized how much my body hurt. Shooting pain seemed to be coming at me from every direction. My skin was throbbing and there was a pulsating pain going though my entire body. I blinked back tears and started swimming toward his family.

I changed my mind. I hated hiking. Hated camping. Hated everything about it. No showers, soiled clothes, bees, everything!

When my feet touched bottom, Tad's mom was in the water next to me. "Are you okay, Allie?" She put her arms around me and hugged me.

Hugged me? Since when did anyone hug me?

I immediately started crying. Bawling. And I couldn't stop.

How totally embarrassing.

"Oh, dear, you're hurt." She kept one arm around me and pulled me to shallow water. "Sit."

I sat, hip deep in water. Tad's mom lifted my leg out of the water and inspected it. Then the other one. Then my arm. Then my other arm. By the time she was finished, I felt like I'd been to the doctor.

Except I hadn't. I was sitting in a lake with Tad's mom taking care of me. It was so weird to have a mom taking care of me. It almost made me want to start bawling again.

"How many bee stings?" Tad asked.

I glanced at him, surprised by the concern in his voice. Sure enough, his eyebrows were furrowed and he looked worried.

"At least eight."

I stared at his mom. "I was stung eight times?"

"At least." She squatted in front of me. "Have you been stung before?"

"Well, sure. But not for a long time." Pain was still radiating through my body, but the tears seemed to have stopped. Thank heaven.

"And are you allergic?"

I shook my head.

"Well, that's good." His mom shot a relieved look at the crew standing on the shore. "I think we're going to be okay."

We. As in, we're all in this together. As a team. I managed a trembling smile.

"There you go, sweetie. Keep smiling." Tad's mom hugged me again. "So, what now? Are you up for heading back?"

"Through the bees?" I couldn't keep the panic out of my voice, and she smiled.

"No. We were going on a loop anyway, so we'll finish it out." She patted my arm. "Unfortunately, there's no fast way back to camp. We're at least two hours away."

Two hours? When my poor body was about to go into shock?

"Maybe we should stop here for lunch," Beth suggested. "Give her time to recover."

No way was I going to ruin everyone's day. I immediately stood up. "No, I'm fine. I can go."

"I'm starving." Tad's dad ignored me. "I was hoping we were going to stop soon."

"Me too." Luke set down the two little ones. "Let's eat."

"No, seriously, I'm okay. You don't need to stop."

I was completely ignored.

"There's a little bit of sand here. It's enough to sit on for lunch." Beth set her backpack on the ground. "Let's eat!"

I stared as the family took ownership of the beach and set up lunch. For me. I wasn't fooled. I was the reason they were stopping, and I was totally overwhelmed.

Tad leaned over my shoulder. "You might want to sit in the water for a while. The coolness will help take some of the heat out."

I twisted around to look at him. "You think?"

He nodded. "I'll sit with you."

And he did. Sat right down in the water next to me.

So I sat down too.

Tad's mom handed me a sandwich, and Tad helped himself to one as well. We were a little away from everyone else, because they were on dry land. After a few minutes, I sort of peeked at Tad. "Um, thanks for saving me."

His cheeks turned red again and he shrugged. "No biggie."

"No, seriously. You could have gotten stung too." I frowned. "Did you get stung?"

"Only once. Not a big deal." He took a bite of his sandwich and looked really uncomfortable.

"You got stung?" For me? He had suffered for me? "Where?"

He held out his arm. A small welt was pulsating on his forearm.

"Tad." I didn't know what to say. No one had ever taken a bee sting for me before.

His cheeks were still flushed, and he shrugged. "How is the sandwich? You like tuna?"

"Yep." I took a bite and chewed and tried not to think about the pain on my cheek and around my right eye. The pain could mean only one thing: that I had at least one sting on my face, and that my cheek and eye were puffing up the way Tad's forearm was. Allie, the beauty queen.

Not.

No makeup. Unstyled hair. Welts on my face. Wearing my sleeping T-shirt.

My friends would never recognize me. I wasn't sure I recognized myself, to be honest.

Chapter Nine

"What song should we sing first?"

I looked at Tad's dad in surprise. "We're going to sing?" We'd finished up dinner about twenty minutes ago, and I was sitting on a blanket with ice packs on my various body parts. Tad was holding the ones on my arm while I held one to my face. Gravity was making nice work of the ice packs on my shins. Luke had actually taken the truck to buy more ice so I'd have enough.

How weird was it to have someone shopping for me? I felt like the queen being pampered.

"Of course. What's camping without some singing around the campfire?" Tad's dad nodded at Luke. "You bring the guitar?"

"Yep." Luke deposited a toddler who I think was named Missy into the lap of another sister-in-law, who I think was named Ruth. "It's in my tent."

There were sixteen people around the campfire. Sixteen people plus me. Sixteen people whom I hadn't known at all twenty-four hours ago, sixteen people who now felt like family. And Tad. I smiled at him, and he grinned back.

Luke reappeared and took a seat on a log as he began strumming. "What do you want to sing?"

"How about 'Supercalifragilisticexpialidocious'?" Beth suggested. "We watched *Mary Poppins* earlier this week on television and the girls loved that song."

Luke nodded. "Everyone know that?" He looked at me. "Allie?"

"Actually, I do." I'd seen it on television this week too, and I'd felt an affinity for those two children who had been ignored by their dad. I needed a Mary Poppins of my own. Well, I would if I were younger. I was old enough to manage on my own now.

"Great." Luke strummed a few cords, and then the group started singing. Some people knew the lyrics more than others, so I sang a little louder to help the stumblers with the words. Even Tad was singing, and he had a pretty nice voice.

When the song was over, I realized everyone was staring at me. Uh-oh. What had I done wrong?

"You can sing." It was Luke who spoke.

"Well, of course. Can't everyone?" I felt extremely uncomfortable with everyone still looking at me like I had a horn sprouting out of my head.

"Not that well," Tad's dad said. "Where'd you learn to sing like that?"

I shifted and moved the ice pack over my eye so I couldn't see half the group anymore. "I don't know. Nowhere. I just sing."

"You haven't had training?" This time it was Tad's mom. What was with the inquisition?

"No." I sounded defensive, but I couldn't help it. "So what? There's nothing wrong with that."

Tad leaned close and I felt his breath on my ear. "My mom is a voice coach. She and my dad both sing in the choir at church. They're very musical."

Oh. So that's why they were so interested.

Tad's mom wasn't finished. "Allie, you have to cultivate that voice. Train it, develop it. It's lovely."

I sort of shrugged. "I don't know." Sure, my friends always told me I could sing, and I knew I could carry a tune, but no one had ever called it out before.

"I'll teach you. Come work with me." Tad's mom looked so excited I wouldn't have been surprised to see her explode straight up into the air off her log.

I shifted. "Um . . . I've never really thought about my singing before."

"You have talent, my dear, and it would be a sin to let that gift go to waste. We'll start training on Monday, okay? Don't bother to answer. It's a done deal." She gave me a firm nod and the rest of the group started to discuss what song to sing next. I just sat there with ice freezing my face.

Me? A singer? With talent? I wasn't an athlete. I didn't care about school. The only thing anyone ever noticed about me was how I filled out my shirts. Until now. With my puffy face and horrible hair, Tad's family still thought I was special.

Unbelievable.

Luke nodded at me. "Since you're the newest musical talent to fall into our circle, you pick the next song."

"Me?"

"Yep."

I looked around and everyone was looking at me, waiting, ready to do what I said. Even Tad. He gave me a wink, and I grinned.

Okay, so maybe I liked camping after all.

Tad and I went for a midnight swim to cool off my bee stings again. We swam out over my head, and then Tad stopped and treaded water. "Can you float on your back?"

"Yes. Why?"

"Do it, and look at the sky."

I glanced up and realized the black sky was dotted with more stars than I'd ever seen in my entire life. I immediately rolled onto my back and puffed up my chest so I didn't sink.

Amazing. I was pretty sure I could see every single star in existence. Did it make me feel insignificant or what?

"Did you see that?" Tad asked.

"See what?"

"The shooting star. Off toward shore."

"No, darn it. I've never seen one." I turned so I could study the sky over the land. "What am I looking for?"

"A streak of light." Tad bumped against my leg. "Sorry."

"No problem." Really. It was no problem. I was beginning to be fond of him touching me, though it had only been to tackle me into the water in a bee rescue and to hold ice on my arm. I wondered what it would be like if he held my hand, just to hold it.

I saw a streak of light and shrieked. "Was that one?"

"Yeah. Cool, huh?"

"Incredible."

We stayed floating forever, and I saw eight shooting stars.

"One for each bee sting," Tad said as we were slogging through the water back to shore.

"Don't remind me."

"Want to sit for a minute?" He nodded at a flat rock on the shore.

My stomach jiggled all of a sudden. "Definitely."

He spread out his towel and we sat next to each other. Not touching. Normally, I'd have no qualms about leaning against him and giving him some broad hints, but I didn't. I had no idea what he was thinking about me. Or why I was having guy/girl thoughts about him.

So we sat in silence for a while, listening to the water lapping at the shore.

"Can I ask you something, Allie?"

"Of course." I crossed my fingers behind my back and hoped it was something good.

"What happened with Rand last night?"

It felt like an eternity had passed since then. "We had a difference of opinion."

"I'd like to hear about it."

I angled my head so I could look at him, but he was staring across the lake. His face was lit by the moon, so his skin was a bluish, grayish, glowing color. "Why?"

"Because."

Because you like me and want to know whether

Rand is out of the picture? I could only hope. On the chance my wish came true, it was worth it to tell Tad what had happened. "He wanted to kiss me, and I didn't want to."

His neck tensed, but he still didn't look at me. "Why not?"

"Um . . ." I chewed my lower lip while I tried to figure out how to explain something I wasn't sure I even understood.

"I thought you liked him."

"I did. Or I thought I did." Didn't I?

"What changed?" He stole a sideways glance at me, then focused on the horizon again.

I rubbed my chin. "I'm not sure. I guess . . . well . . . I'm tired of people ditching me."

"What makes you think he would have ditched you?"

I rolled my eyes. "Give me a break. I'm the queen of short relationships. I look for that kind of guy, and Rand is the perfect specimen. No attention span, which is exactly what I wanted."

Tad finally gave up the pretense of not listening and turned to look at me. "So, if he's perfect, why'd you dunk him? Playing hard to get?"

"No." I pursed my lips. "I'm just sick of being ditched."

We were quiet for a moment.

"Who ditched you?"

I hugged my knees to my chest. "My dad."

He made a noise of sympathy. "What happened? Divorce?"

"Well, yeah, but that's not the problem. He took off for California, and I haven't spent very much time with him in six years. I was supposed to go out and stay with him for the summer and get to know the woman he's going to marry, but then he called the night before I was supposed to leave and disinvited me." I bit my lip. Jerk.

"That sucks."

I couldn't help but laugh at his emphatic tone. "I know." Then I sobered. "Most people think it's cool that I have no parental supervision. My friends tell me all the time how lucky I am that my mom is never home and no one cares if I stay out all night."

"It has its advantages," Tad said. "But it sucks to be ditched by your parents." He was quiet for a moment. "You know my dad?"

"Uh-huh. He's really nice."

"He's not my real dad."

I could have fallen off the rock in shock at that comment. "Are you serious? But he seems so close with everyone, and your mom. And you. He seems to really love you."

Tad threw a rock into the lake and watched it skip. "He does. He married my mom ten years ago, so he's the only dad I know. My own dad never comes around. My older brothers remember him, but I don't. Not much, at least."

How about that? Someone else with a dad who pulled the disappearing act. "Don't you want to meet him? To see him?"

"Nope. He's not my dad anymore." He threw another rock, and it landed with a blurp, then disappeared under the surface. "If your dad doesn't care about you, he's not your dad. Don't let him mess with you." He shrugged. "Maybe your mom will marry someone else like my mom did."

I thought of evil Jack and his usurping daughter.

"Or not. But at least you still have her."

"Well, sort of. Dating is more important than me." But what if she was out looking for a dad for me? What if she was actually trying to take care of me?

Nah. She was too selfish for that.

"Then come hang at my house. My family loves you."

Warmth settled in my belly. "Really?" *What about you?*

"Yep. You heard them. My mom already has you

on her list of potential superstars that she has to mold into greatness."

Greatness? There was the possibility of greatness in my future? "Maybe I will."

He nodded.

So . . . what now?

"Ready to head up?"

"Sure."

Tad hopped down and took my hand to help me jump off, but then he let go once I was on the ground. He walked me to my tent, then sort of stood there for a minute. "So, um, tomorrow we head back."

"Back to real life."

He nodded. "Back to carrots and tomatoes."

My stomach turned to sludge at the thought. What if he returned to the old Tad? "Tad?"

He was watching me closely, and I shifted under his gaze. "What?"

"Are you going to be mean again on Monday?"

He lifted a brow. "What are you talking about?"

"Well, you were pretty impatient with me when we were at work. Nothing like how you've been up here." Gah. How pathetic did I sound? I was a major loser. As if whether Tad was nice or not could affect me. "I mean, whatever."

His hand went toward my arm, but he dropped it

before he actually touched me. "I thought you were different from how you are. I misjudged you."

Was it good or bad that he had changed his opinion? I was afraid to ask.

"We'll be cool."

Cool? What did that mean? Why didn't he just grab me and kiss me and tell me he was so glad I wasn't interested in Rand because he couldn't live without me?

He touched my shoulder. "See you in the morning."

"In the morning." Yeah, that was so romantic.

Then he turned away and walked off to his tent. Gave me a little wave, then disappeared through the flaps.

Never had I wanted a boy to kiss me more, and never had I felt more at a loss for how to let him know. Or maybe he did know, and he didn't care. Or maybe he did know and the thought repulsed him.

For the first time in my life, I needed my friends' advice on boys. Badly.

We were sitting on Blue's bed eating popcorn while I filled Natalie, Blue and Frances in on the entire weekend. I did a little show-and-tell with my faded welts from the bee stings, and got appropriate sympathy for the sorry fate of all my cute clothes.

I'd had Tad's parents drop me off at Blue's house. Why would I want to go home to an empty house? After being around so many people all weekend, it would have been too lonely.

"So, you totally like him?" Natalie whooped and raised her arms over her head in a sign of victory. "I knew it!"

I grinned. "I owe you."

"Darn right you do. Do you have any idea how torturous it was to ride with Rand for four hours? The guy has a major ego. He even made a move on me." She rolled her eyes and flopped on the bed. "I have no idea how he and Tad are related."

I didn't have to ask anymore whether Natalie liked Tad. The fact she'd taken off with Rand was enough of an answer, but I really did owe her. Big time.

Frances held up her hand. "So, let me get this straight. You went swimming with him in your bikini at night alone and he didn't try to kiss you? Not even on the cheek?"

"Yep."

"Why didn't he try to kiss you?"

"How am I supposed to know? Probably doesn't like me."

Blue and Frances exchanged hopeful glances, and I threw a pillow at them. "Can't you forget

154

about your bet? This is my happiness we're talking about."

Blue shook her head. "Sorry, but stuffing my bra takes priority. I have to avoid public humiliation at all costs."

Stupid bet. I needed all the support I could get. "Let's scrap the bet. Please. I need help."

"No way!" Natalie sat up. "They're about to go down, so you can't let them off the hook. We'll totally manage this on our own."

I eyed Blue and Frances, who weren't looking too worried. "How do we know they won't sabotage things?"

"Because deep down inside they're your friends and would never hurt you." Natalie sounded so confident I almost believed her. "But I do think we need to kick them out if we're going to discuss plans for snaring Tad."

"No way." Blue folded her arms. "We won't interfere, but it's only fair if we know what we're up against."

Natalie stood up. "Sorry, but there's no chance. Allie, let's go to your house." She nodded at Frances and Blue. "We'll see you guys at work tomorrow."

They grumbled and complained, but Natalie wouldn't let them deter her (and me) from our exit.

As we walked down the street toward my house, each of us carrying one of my bags from the weekend, I felt increasingly morose.

I didn't want to go home.

Especially when we turned the corner and saw a car in my driveway that didn't belong to my mom.

Chapter Ten

"Whose car is that?" Natalie asked.

"I don't know." I took my key out of my bag. "We'll sneak in the back door and go up to my room."

Unfortunately, we hadn't even made it to the house before the front door opened and my mom appeared on the porch. "Allie! Natalie! You're just in time for dinner."

I narrowed my eyes. Since when did my mom cook dinner? "Whose car is that?"

"Come on in." My mom stood back and held the door for us.

I had no choice but to go inside, but it was the last thing I wanted to do. I kept Natalie close and we stepped into the front hall.

"To the dining room." She took our elbows and guided us to the back of the house.

We stepped into the room and there was a man who looked as old as my mom, and a girl who looked like she was my age, only she wasn't dressed fashionably. She was wearing a flowered button-down shirt and had her hair in some weird curly thing and she had no makeup on.

"Allie, this is my friend Jack and his daughter Martha."

Jack and Martha at my house? At my dining-room table? My mom had totally betrayed me. How dare she spring this on me?

She put an arm around my shoulders and another around Natalie's. "This is my daughter Allie, and her friend Natalie Page."

I was surprised she could still remember Natalie's name, it had been so long since she'd been around any of my friends.

Jack immediately stood up and gave me a smothering hug that made me want to vomit. Then Martha smiled. "Hi, Allie. I'm really glad to meet you."

I couldn't say the same, Little Miss Mom-Stealer. For Jack and Martha, my mom cooked. For me? Microwave pizza if I was lucky.

"Hi," Natalie said. "What's for dinner?"

"Grilled salmon," my mom said. "Plenty for all. I was hoping you two would be stopping by."

Grilled salmon. A gourmet feast by my mom's standards. Obviously, Jack and Martha were on a pedestal way above me. "I have to go unpack."

"You can do that after dinner."

"I have to wash my clothes."

My mom narrowed her eyes at me. "After dinner."

"I have to go put lotion on my eight bee stings."

That got a moment's pause. "You have eight bee stings?"

Natalie bobbed her head. "You can still see the marks."

I pointed to my cheek.

My mom leaned closer to look, and then her face sort of crumpled. "I didn't notice."

"Big surprise."

"I'm sorry, hon."

"About the bee stings or not noticing?"

"Both."

That was a new one. My mom apologizing for not noticing me? Probably for the benefit of our guests. "I'll eat upstairs."

Her sad look morphed into Killer Amazon Woman. "You *will* be eating with us."

I glared at her.

"And you *will* be pleasant."

"Or what? You'll ground me? Then you'd have

to curtail your social life to make sure I was staying home."

"Allie."

"What?" I was being belligerent. So what? I wasn't proud of it, but I couldn't help it. She wanted me to sit down with the very people who had stolen from me what little bit of her I had? As if.

"Sit down or I will call Mr. Novak tomorrow and tell him you won't be working for him this summer."

"Mom! You can't do that!" Take away my job? My time with Tad and my friends? Next she'd probably ban me from taking singing lessons with Tad's mom.

"Can't I?"

I glared at her, and she scowled right back. She'd won, and we both knew it.

Planting my butt in the chair next to Natalie, I promised myself that even if I had to be polite, I wasn't going to mean it and I wasn't going to enjoy it.

So there.

I was already out in the strawberry fields when Tad showed up to work. I was wearing an outfit that was perfect for the farm. Old jeans, old sneakers (I'd had to dig in the back of my closet and then run them through some mud to make them suitable), a blue farm stand T-shirt and a baseball cap. Minimum makeup and my hair in a natural ponytail with no curling iron benefit.

Natalie and I had decided that since Tad had seemed to respond to me once I got ugly camping, maybe that was the right thing to do to get him to notice me as a girl. I felt weird and ugly, but also sort of liberated. It had taken me no time to get ready this morning, since I hadn't had to do my hair or makeup.

"Hi, Allie." Tad dropped to his knees next to me. "How you doing?"

I smiled at him and leaned back on my heels. "Good, now that you're here." His smile faltered, and I quickly added, "Because you can help me with the work." Darn it. Why did he look so panicked at the thought that I might like him? Were Frances and Blue right? Did he really not like me in that way?

"Right." He set up his basket and started working next to me in silence, picking the strawberries twice as fast as I was.

Bowl me over. This wasn't exactly the passionate greeting I'd been hoping for. What was wrong with me? I was dressed the way he liked, I was working hard.

"So, my mom wants you to come home with me

after work sometime so you can do the singing thing. Maybe on Wednesday?" he said.

A glimmer of excitement ran through me—though it was only a glimmer due to the fact that I was very aware the invite had been phrased as coming from his mother, not from him. "Do you mind if I come home with you?"

He shrugged. "It's fine."

Fine.

Fine.

Fine?

Sure, he was working next to me and being nice instead of giving me annoyed looks and staying at the other end of the field, so that was good, right? But he wouldn't compliment me on my outfit or even act like he wanted me to go home with him?

I slammed a strawberry into the basket, then glared at its splattered remains. Blue and Frances were right. He didn't even like me.

Unbelievable.

"Did you have fun camping this weekend?" Tad asked.

"Yeah." I glared at the basket, yanked out the strawberry bits and hucked them into the dirt. Take that, stupid strawberry!

"Do your bee stings still hurt?"

I sighed. Why was he asking me that? It almost sounded like he cared, and I couldn't deal with that. "They're okay."

"Did you get the orange juice out of your clothes?"

"I haven't tried." I'd spent the night entertaining Jack and Martha. I hated them both, even though they hadn't done anything wrong or offensive.

"Hey!"

I looked at him. "What?"

"What's your problem?"

"My problem?" I dropped the strawberries into the basket and put my hands on my hips? "*My* problem?"

"Yeah. You're giving me one-word answers to everything. I'm trying to have a conversation with you."

I blinked. "You are?"

"Of course I am. You think I'm talking to myself?"

He was talking to me. That was an improvement over our pre-camping relationship, wasn't it?

"Allie." He touched my arm. "What's bugging you? Did something happen last night after we dropped you off?"

My biggest problem at the moment was that I wanted him to like me and he was showing no inclination of that. But my second problem was close behind. "Actually, yeah. I went home and my mom had invited her boyfriend and his daughter over for dinner. I had to spend the night with them."

He lifted a brow. "Well, that's good, isn't it? You could get a new dad?"

"No, it's not good! She's been totally abandoning me lately so she can spend time with them. Do you realize she has gone to that girl's softball games, but she can't even find time to spend with her own daughter the night before she's supposed to leave for the entire summer? She loves them more than me, and now she wants me to welcome them into my life." I bit back tears and stared at the green leaves peeping out of the dirt. What was I doing telling Tad about this? I didn't talk about this stuff with anyone. To do so would seriously interfere with my totally-with-it-and-together persona that I project.

Tad sat back on his heels. "When my mom first started dating my dad, my brothers hated him. I was too small to care, but I remember hearing them complain and moan."

"I can't believe that. Your dad is so awesome."

Tad shrugged. "We didn't know it back then. To us, he was an outsider trying to mess up our family."

"I guess." Tad's dad was awesome. I loved him. If

he were the guy my mom was dating, I'd be okay with that.

"Maybe this guy will be like my dad. Maybe he's nice."

"Or maybe he's stealing my mom from me."

"Maybe you should give him a chance."

"Or not." How could I give Jack and his weaselley daughter a chance? It was already clear that there was no room for me in that little trio. "Maybe you should butt out."

He lifted a brow. "If that's what you want."

I frowned as I watched him walk away and set up about ten yards from me. I didn't want him to butt out, did I? I certainly didn't need someone telling me what to do about my mom and her love toy. And I didn't need to waste time on a boy who didn't like me.

I did kinda want to learn how to sing though. How cool would it be to actually have talent at something?

What would Tad think of me if I had talent? Not that I'd do it for him. Or anyone.

It would be for myself.

I got Tad's phone number from Mr. Novak, and I called his mom on my lunch break to arrange a time for lessons. She didn't take credit cards, so I was going to have to figure that one out. I didn't have a checking account, and she preferred not to take cash for tax purposes, she'd said.

We agreed to meet on Wednesday after work. I told her I'd take a cab to her house, but she said that Rand could drive me since he'd be coming home with Tad anyway.

I'd take the cab.

For the rest of day, I kept finding myself humming, even when Tad ate lunch with Natalie instead of me, and even when Rand averted his eyes when he passed me next to the mulch pile.

I didn't need them anymore. I had my own talent.

Ha.

The next step was to convince myself of that fact. Both facts, actually. That I didn't need them, and that I had my own talent.

Neither fact seemed too likely, actually.

"Allie? You coming?" Rand was in his truck, Tad in the passenger seat, and the engine was running.

I shook my head. "Nope. I'm all set."

"Mom said you were coming to our house for voice lessons, and that I was to give you a ride."

Voice lessons. How cool did that sound? "I'm taking a cab."

"A cab? Are you kidding?"

"Nope." I sat down on one of the logs lining the parking lot. "It'll be here in a minute."

Rand turned to Tad, and they chatted for a sec, and I tried not to care what they might be saying about me. Then Tad got out and came around the truck to stand in front of me. "Allie?"

I looked past him, willing the cab to round the corner. "What?"

"Are you mad at me?"

Not the question I'd been expecting. I thought he was going to order me into the truck, to which I had my retort well thought out. But whether I was mad at him? I didn't think he'd even noticed me all week, and today I'd gone back to dressing cute again. Practical, but still cute.

Hadn't made a difference. He still hadn't paid any attention to me.

"Why would I be mad at you?" *Other than the fact that you don't care that I exist.*

"Because of what I said about that guy your mom is dating." He shifted. "I didn't mean to make you mad. I thought maybe I could help since I'd gone through the same thing."

I hadn't thought of it that way before. Maybe that's why I'd confided in Tad—because he could understand. And maybe, just maybe, that gave him a little bit of leeway in giving me advice. I sighed. "I guess I'm not mad at you."

He grinned and held out his hand. "Then let's go. Forget the cab."

At that moment, the cab pulled into the parking lot. Tad pulled me to my feet, then walked over to the cab and said something to the driver, who then drove off.

And I let him. I didn't jump in front of him and tell him I could make my own decisions.

For once, it felt okay to have someone help me out. Especially if that someone was Tad. I think he got me. I mean, really got me.

He opened the passenger door to the truck. "Coming?"

"Now that you sent away my ride, I guess I have no choice."

He grinned. "Exactly. You want shotgun?"

I lowered my voice so only he could hear. "And sit next to your brother? Not a chance."

His smile got bigger, and he nodded. "I always knew you were a smart girl."

No chance I was smart. I smiled as I climbed into the backseat. But apparently, I could sing.

I couldn't wait for my first lesson.

But as I sat in the back of the truck and watched

Tad and Rand chat, I couldn't help but wonder if I had any hope at all with Tad.

Despite all my best efforts, I cared.

Darn it.

I was going to have to do something about my soft side.

Chapter Eleven

Was it possible to adopt an entire family?

My voice lesson had been awesome, then Mrs. Novak had invited me to stay for dinner. Mr. Novak had come home at six and played hoops with Tad and Rand for a while, then Beth and Luke had come over with their little ones.

Everyone was so nice and welcomed me, and I never wanted to leave.

But it was almost nine and I couldn't stay any longer. "I should go." Would someone please throw themselves at my feet and beg me to stay forever?

"Do you want to call your mom and have her come get you now?" Tad's mom asked.

It was too far to walk home from here, but ask my mom to come get me? I started to say I'd take a cab, but the words died in my throat. I didn't want them to know what a dysfunctional family I had. I wanted them to think of me as one of them, normal and loved. "Yeah, I'll try calling her."

I punched in the number of my mom's cell phone and crossed my fingers that once, just once, she'd answer.

And amazingly enough, she did. "Allie! Where are you?"

"Can you give me a ride home?"

"From where? I've been worried sick about you since you didn't come home from work."

I blinked. "What?"

"I thought you usually get home around four o'clock, don't you? I called the farm stand and they said you'd gotten off work at three. It's past nine! I called Blue and Natalie and Frances, and you weren't at any of their houses. Where are you?"

I had to sit down I was so shocked. "Since when do you keep track of when I come home?"

"Don't start with me, young lady. Tell me where you are. We'll talk when I get there."

This was amazing. My mom had actually noticed I was gone. How cool was that?

"Allie? Where are you?"

"At a friend's house." Suddenly, I didn't want to tell her why I was here. With her recent decision to play the mom role, I was afraid she'd pull rank and ban me from voice lessons.

"Where?"

I realized I had no idea. "Hang on. Let me get someone." I walked into the kitchen, where Tad's mom and dad were cleaning up from dinner. "Can one of you give my mom directions?"

"I'll do that." Tad's mom wiped her hands on a towel, then took the phone and disappeared into the other room.

So I picked up her towel and finished drying the pot she'd been working on. Tad's dad shot me a look, then handed me a pan he'd just rinsed.

I dried. He washed. We chatted about my school and my friends.

How could Tad's brothers have hated this man? He was awesome.

What if Jack was this cool?

No, I hated Jack.

Didn't I?

Tad walked into the kitchen, and I smiled at him. He smiled back. "You sounded great."

My cheeks immediately became hot. "Shut up."

"No, you did." He took the dry pan out of my hand. "You're a great singer."

"You weren't supposed to be listening."

He grinned and set the pan in a cabinet under the stove. "I eavesdropped. I wanted to see if you were as good as my mom thought you were."

"I'm not, am I?"

"Better."

My cheeks got even hotter. "Liar."

"Nope."

Tad's dad finished washing and slipped out of the kitchen.

I handed Tad a mixing bowl I'd finished drying. "Are you serious? Do you really think I'm good?" I held my breath as I waited for his answer. I *really* wanted him to say yes. I wanted to be special in some way.

"Yes."

I couldn't stop the huge grin from spreading across my face. "Cool."

"So . . . um . . . this thing with you and Rand is totally over, huh?"

"Of course it is. I told you that in Maine."

"Right. Just checking."

Why was he checking? Why? Why? Why?

"You always date older guys, huh?" He put the mixing bowl above the stove and didn't look at me.

"I don't date much."

He looked at me sharply. "I don't believe that."

"It's true." With no more dishes to dry, I set the

towel on the table. Kissing random boys at parties didn't count as dating. "I don't like to get involved."

"Oh."

"Usually. There's always room for exceptions." I held my breath and waited.

"Is there?" He leaned against the counter and folded his arms across his chest. "What kind of exceptions?"

"I might be willing to get involved if it was a guy I liked." *Come on, Tad! Do you need any more hints than this?* I wasn't going to come right out and tell him. What if he rejected me? Sure, I liked him, but a girl has to have her pride.

He studied me. "Interesting."

Interesting? That was all he had to say?

"Is there any guy in particular that you like at the moment?"

I met his gaze. "Maybe."

"Allie! Your mom's here!"

Argh! Of all the times for her to actually show an interest in my life, it had to be *now?*

Tad levered himself off the counter. "Let's go."

Let's go? He couldn't take a moment to declare his interest in me? It would only take one second.

Obviously, he didn't want to make any declarations, which led to the conclusion that he didn't actually like me in that way.

"Fine. Let's go." I left him standing in the kitchen and walked to the front hall, where Mrs. Novak was telling my mom about my incredible singing talent. So much for keeping it a secret. If my mom tried to stop me from taking voice lessons, I'd run away. "Hi, Mom."

Her gaze swiveled to me, and I was startled to see the look of sadness on her face. "Allie." She folded me into a huge hug and held me for a long minute.

When was the last time she'd hugged me? Maybe when I was born?

She kept one arm around my shoulders even after she released me. Tad was standing in the doorway, a thoughtful expression on his face. What was he thinking? I totally wished I could read minds right now. Or did I? Did I really want to know if he was thinking that I was so not his type?

Maybe I did. At least then I could move on. Yes, I did want to know. It was the only way to get my control and independence back. Maybe I'd ask him tomorrow at work.

Better yet, I'd get Natalie to ask him. That was a much better plan.

My mom finished her farewells and her thank-yous, and even wrote a check to Mrs. Novak.

Did that mean she was going to let me sing?

WHO NEEDS BOYS?

I crossed my fingers behind my back as I followed her out of the house. And when I turned to get into the car, I noticed Tad and his mom were both standing on the porch.

Natalie was definitely going to have to talk to Tad tomorrow. I couldn't stand not knowing how he felt anymore.

"Why didn't you tell me you were taking singing lessons?"

I dragged my thoughts from Tad and looked at my mom. "I didn't think you'd care."

She nodded as she turned out onto the street. "Why would you think that?" Her voice was soft, not angry or accusatory.

So I answered her. "Because you don't have time for me anymore. You only care about Jack and his daughter."

She shot a glance at me. "You know that's not true."

"Do I? You go to her softball games, you make dinner for them, you leave me home alone every night so you can go hang out with them. I eat microwave pizza, and you cook salmon for them. What else am I supposed to think?"

My mom was quiet for a long time.

In fact, neither of us said anything more for the entire ride home, and that totally bummed me out.

I wanted her to leap up and deny what I'd said. To announce that she loved me more than anything and that Jack and Martha meant nothing to her.

But she'd been silent. Which meant I was right. And that gave me a lot to think about.

My mom flicked on the light in the kitchen and nodded at the kitchen table. "Sit. We need to talk."

That we did.

I sat, and once she had taken the seat opposite me, I made my announcement. "Blue's parents said I could move in with them for the summer. I've decided I'm going to do that."

My mom looked at me. "Why?"

"Because they care about me." I blinked against the tears that burned at the back of my eyes.

"I love you, Allie."

"No, you don't. Neither does Dad."

She sighed and looked very tired. "Yes, he does."

"How can you say that?" My voice was getting high now, but I didn't care. "He's barely seen me in six years, and then when I was supposed to go see him, he changes his mind because he has to take care of his fiancée. And now you're hanging out with Jack and his daughter. There's no room for me in either of your lives, and I don't want to be here anymore."

"Allie . . ."

I shook my head and stood up. Tears were streaming down my face, but I didn't care. "Do you have any idea what it was like to be with Tad's family this weekend? They love each other, they make time for each other. They took care of me! Do you realize his mom made dinner for me and tended to me when I got stung? When was the last time anyone did that for me, huh? When?" I was screaming so loudly my throat hurt.

My mom stood up, grabbed my shoulders and hauled me against her. "I'm so sorry, honey."

"Let go of me!" I tried to push her off, but she held me tighter.

"I love you, Allie. I'm so sorry for what I've done to you." I felt her kiss my hair, and she hugged me tighter. "I'm so sorry," she said again.

And I cried.

I mean, I really cried. Harder than I've ever cried. I tried to fight her off, but she wouldn't let go of me. So I finally gave up and cried on her. Served her right if I ruined her beautiful blouse.

After I couldn't cry anymore, I pushed away from her. Then I got the shock of my life. She'd been crying too. Tears were still streaming down her cheeks and her eyes were all red.

I had no idea how to respond. Moms weren't supposed to cry.

She gave me this teary smile and patted my chair. So I sat, and she did too. Then she handed me a tissue box, and we both blew our noses and wiped mascara off our cheeks.

It was almost a bonding moment.

"Allie."

"What?"

"I will always love you more than anyone or anything." She held up her hand to silence me before I could protest. "I know I haven't done a good job of showing it. And Jack and his daughter can't ever replace you. I'll always love you more. But I know how much it hurts that your dad has left, and I wanted more than anything to find you someone else. Another dad. Not to replace yours, but in addition."

I swallowed the lump in my throat and thought of Tad's dad.

"It's no excuse for how I've abandoned you, but I've been trying to find you a dad, and someone for me. You're lonely, but so am I. I wanted to find us a family."

A family? I wanted a family. Especially after being around Tad's. I didn't realize my mom wanted one too. I'd never actually thought about the fact that she might be as sad as I was about my dad leaving. Maybe I should have.

"I really think you might like Jack and Martha, but if you don't, I wouldn't force them on you. But it's because I love you that I want you to give them a chance."

Again, Tad's dad came to mind.

She took my hand and rubbed the back of it. "I feel horrible that I never thought of giving you voice lessons. I've been a terrible mom, and I can't tell you how much I regret it." She started crying again, and I didn't know what to do. I mean, I couldn't exactly tell her she'd been a great mom, could I?

There was one thing I could do, though. "I'll give Jack and Martha a chance. As long as you spend more time with me."

She nodded and held my hand tightly. "It's a deal, Allie."

"And can I take voice lessons?"

"Of course! I'll drive you there as often as you want."

I thought of catching a ride with Tad and Rand. "Tell you what. Give me a day to figure things out. Maybe I'll only need a ride home."

My mom sort of gave me a look. "You like Tad?"

I felt my cheeks get hot. "I don't know."

"He's a lucky boy. You're very special."

"You think I'm special?" I couldn't quite manage not to make my voice trembly.

The hug she gave me convinced me that she did. After she finished persuading me, she got out some ice cream and a couple of bowls and set it up for us on the table. Then she grinned. "Tell me all about Tad. I'm dying to know."

I stuck my spoon in the ice cream. "I don't think he likes me."

"Why?"

I spent the next hour filling her in about Tad and Rand and camping and work. By the time I was finished, my mom was certain Tad liked me.

Did I hope she was right, or what? Tomorrow, I'd find out when Natalie asked him.

I wasn't sure I was ready for the answer.

Chapter Twelve

Natalie stopped picking strawberries, folded her arms across her chest and shook her head. "No. I won't ask him."

"But you have to! I can't handle not knowing." How could she do this to me?

"Ask him yourself."

"Why?"

"Because it's the right thing to do."

"But I can't. What if he says no to my face? I'll be totally embarrassed."

"And what if he says yes? I'll tell you, and then you two will give each other nervous looks for the next two weeks, afraid to actually talk to each other now that you know how the other feels. It's better if you do it." She rolled her eyes. "You're tough, Allie. You can handle it."

I bit my lip. Sometimes there was a definite disadvantage to putting on that persona. Tad knew it wasn't true, yet he liked me anyway. Well, liked, not *liked.*

"Morning." Tad dropped his wheelbarrow with a thud and nodded at us.

He was wearing his usual outfit, khaki shorts and a T-shirt and hat. He was so cute I could barely stand it.

I had decided to wear my farm stand T-shirt, jeans that were old but still fashionable and trendy sneakers. Light makeup and my hair only partially pulled back, but I hadn't used the curling iron. More casual than I was at the beginning of the summer by a lot, but still good enough that Tad had to notice, right?

Natalie studied both of us, and I wondered if she'd changed her mind. "I'm going to go get another shovel," I suggested, to see if she'd stay and talk to Tad. *Come on, Natalie. Do it, please.*

She eyed me, then looked at Tad. "You two need to get things sorted out on your own."

"Natalie!"

"Tad, Allie likes you. Tad, if you like her, tell her. If not, put her out of her misery. Have a nice day." And then she took off running toward the shed. Good thing she was fast because I would have shoved my work gloves down her throat if she wasn't already across the field.

My cheeks were roasting and I couldn't look at Tad. So I kneeled down in the dirt and started digging. I had no idea what I was digging for, and I wasn't anywhere near a plant, but I didn't care. Anything not to look like a total idiot.

Then Tad kneeled in front of me. "Is that true?"

I couldn't look at him. "She's making it up."

"So you don't like me?"

I shoved hard at the dirt. "I didn't at first. You were a jerk."

"Yeah, sorry about that. Want to know why?"

"No. Yes. Whatever."

"Because a girl like you would never be interested in me."

My head snapped up at that. "What?"

He nodded. "You're beautiful. Obviously very popular, and guys like Rand were all over you. What chance did I have?"

"Did you want a chance?" Shoot. Did I sound too hopeful?

"Of course I did."

Wow.

"So I decided not to like you, so I wouldn't care when you ended up with Rand."

I sat back on my heels. "You did a good job of it."

He shook his head. "No, I didn't. I cared."

I grinned. "Really?"

"Uh-huh."

"So, then, how come when Rand and I didn't work out, you didn't do anything?" Could you have gotten a more romantic setting than the lake at night looking at the stars?

"Because I didn't want to be a consolation prize."

Male pride. So annoying.

"If Rand wanted you back, would you go?"

I rolled my eyes. "You're such a guy. Give it up, Tad. Either like me or don't. You know that I'm the one who shoved Rand on his butt. Yes, I like you, though I can't imagine why because you're a jerk and you torture me."

He was still sitting there watching me.

So I lightly punched him on the shoulder and caught him off balance. Another push and he was on his rear end. "I can't deal with you."

"Then it's mutual. I can't deal with you either."

"Fine. Forget it." I picked up my shovel and climbed to my feet. My legs were shaking and I was so upset I could barely stand, but I wasn't about to let him see that. He might know I was a softy about my dad, but no way was I going to let him find out I was a softy about him.

I had only made it about three feet in my flight when I felt his hand on my wrist. "Wait a sec, Allie."

I stopped, but didn't turn around to face him. "What?"

"I'm sorry."

"About what? Not liking me? Don't worry about it. I didn't really like you anyway. It was part of a bet with my friends." Spiteful, sure, but who needs boys anyway? It was time I showed that I didn't.

He turned me to face him. "What bet?"

"A bet with my friends. Natalie thought that you liked me even though you were a jerk. Blue and Frances said that some boys were actually immune to me, so after they met you, they decided you were one of them, and they bet that you didn't like me. The bet will be over at the end of the summer."

He lifted a brow. "What did you bet?"

"Natalie drafted me, but I thought it was stupid. I don't care enough what you think to make a bet on it." I folded my arms across my chest and tried to look bored. How could I have told him about the bet? It would totally feed his ego, and there should be none of that.

"What happens to the losers?"

Yeah, looked liked I was going to be paying that off. "The losers have to stuff their bras at the first dance of the year. Really stuff them. Giant boobs. As humiliating as possible." I sighed. Like it wasn't bad enough to be rejected by Tad, I had to publicly embarrass myself on top of that?

"Then I guess Frances and Blue will have to go buy bigger bras."

I blinked. "What?"

He just grinned. Then he put his hands on my shoulders and kissed me. On the lips!

How cool was that, huh?

His lips were so soft, like velvet, and his breath smelled like mint. It was the most perfect kiss I'd ever had, and I knew I'd never be the same. Ever.

I guess I needed boys after all. Well, not boys. One particular boy.

Who'd have thunk it?

I heard a shriek from the other end of the field, and we both turned to see Natalie waving. Frances and Blue were standing next to her, and they didn't look happy.

Tad grinned and slung his arm over my shoulder. "I don't think Blue and Frances are going to like me."

I leaned against him and thought about how

perfectly I fit under his arm. "Who cares? They'll get over it. Besides, we ought to thank them. If Natalie wasn't trying to win the bet, she wouldn't have gotten us to go camping and she wouldn't have left with Rand." I looked at him. "We owe her, you know. She suffered with Rand for the entire ride home. Do you have any friends we could set her up with?"

He turned me toward him and slipped his hands around my waist. "I'm not sure I want you around my friends. What if one of them steals you away?"

I linked my hands around his neck and gave him my most brilliant smile. "There's no way."

He grinned. "You sound like you mean that."

"As long as you keep hosing me off, making fun of my clothes and saving me from bees, I'm all yours. Oh, and you have to keep kissing me from time to time." I felt my cheeks heat up. "I like it when you kiss me."

He nodded. "I can live with those terms. Especially the kissing thing." And then he made it clear exactly how easily he could live with the kissing thing.

Did I tell you this was going to be the best summer ever, or what? Obviously, I'm psychic.

* * *

"Who wants watermelon?" I held up a platter as I walked out my back door.

"I'll take some." Tad took the platter from me and carried it to the picnic table where Jack, Martha and my mom were sitting. "Allie's an expert watermelon carver," he said. "You guys are in the presence of greatness."

I grinned at him. How could I not like this guy? Not only did he think I could sing, but everything I did impressed him.

Except when I tried to put too much fertilizer on the raspberries and almost killed them. He wasn't too impressed with that.

What can I say? I'm not an expert. But he likes me anyway, whether I'm dressed up or not. (We did have that discussion, by the way—about why he seemed to disdain me when I tried to look nice. He said that he had been intimidated by me when I was all decked out, and that I was still supercute when I didn't have makeup on. He got a kiss for that comment.)

Tad sat down at the picnic table on the end of the bench, and I climbed in beside him, next to my mom.

I took a bite of one of the burgers, which Jack had cooked. "This is good, Jack."

He smiled at me. "Thanks." It struck me that he

had a very kind smile. His eyes were sort of crinkly and warm. "So, when's your first concert, Allie?"

I sort of shuddered. "Next Wednesday. It's not a concert. It's sort of a recital thing."

"Mind if we come?"

I looked at my mom, and she smiled. Then I looked back at Jack. "You want to come?"

"Of course."

"Me too," Martha said.

I stared at her. "Why would you want to come to a boring recital?"

"Because it's cool that you can sing." She sort of looked embarrassed. "But if you don't want me there, I don't have to come."

My mom stepped on my foot, but it was unnecessary. "No, it would be great if you came."

Martha sort of smiled. "Really?"

"On one condition."

"What?" She looked worried, and I almost laughed.

"You let me do your makeup and your hair beforehand. And maybe you can borrow some of my clothes." If Martha was going to start being seen with me in public, I was going to have to do something about her appearance. And her self-confidence. The clothes and makeup would help, but really, it was all about what she had on the inside, and I could tell she needed a boost of girl power. I was still learning, but I was willing to share what I knew.

Her eyes widened. "Really? You'd help me?"

"Help you? You *want* help?"

She nodded furiously. "That would be awesome. Thanks."

I couldn't believe how happy she looked. Didn't she have any girlfriends to primp and gossip with before heading out? Then I looked at Jack. He was nice, but he was a man. I might not have a dad, but Martha didn't have a mom. "Maybe I'll come to one of your games. You said you play field hockey in the fall?"

"Yes."

Under the table, Tad laced his fingers through mine. "I'm coming on Wednesday too," he said.

I grinned at him. "I figured you might."

"Am I too predictable?"

"No way." I gave him a secret smile that promised a kiss when we were alone.

Not that we were alone much, now that my mom was taking her job as a mom more seriously again. Of course, Jack was usually around too, with Martha, and you know what?

It wasn't half bad.

Not bad at all.

WHO NEEDS BOYS?

Not that we were a family, by any means, but we were becoming friends. My mom was way happier, making me realize that she really hadn't been happy before when she was dating all the guys and was never home. Both of us happy with one guy. How funny was that? And we were beginning to build our own home again.

It was a start, and it was okay. Maybe even a little better than okay.

Who'd have guessed?

Stephie Davis
STUDYING BOYS

HOMEWORK: 0
BOYS: 1

So I study. A lot.

So I have a huge crush on the "wrong guy."

Those two little things justify
my friends blackmailing me?
"Meet some other boys or else...."
Hah. What kind of friends are those?

The kind who can get me grounded.

And get me noticed by that "wrong guy,"
who is actually a jerk and no longer my crush.

Or is he?

⚲ STEPHIE DAVIS ⚲

PUTTING BOYS ON THE LEDGE

You like a boy, but he blows you off. You're bummed out. Guess what? You're on The Ledge. It's a rotten place to be, which is why boys belong out there, not girls! Keep boys out on The Ledge and they'll never be able to hurt you.

Why would Blue Waller want to put a gorgeous senior on The Ledge just when he's starting to notice her? But if she doesn't, will he end up breaking her heart?

Blue—that's short for Blueberry—is cursed with the worst name on the planet, parents that seriously hamper her social life, and the figure of her eight-year-old sister. Good thing she has three best friends to help her find true love—even if it means braving The Ledge.

SUPER ★
★ WHAT?
JAX ABBOTT

**THE TOP FIVE WAYS NOT TO START
YOUR FIRST DAY AT A NEW HIGH SCHOOL:**

1. Tell the hottest guy in class
that he reminds you of an elf.
2. Get *enormongo* cramps.
3. Annoy one of the Populars.
4. Make even the geeks pity you.
5. Finally get the superpowers
you thought you'd *never* have and
explode all the windows in English class.

Jessie was SO not wearing tights and a cape!

- -

EYELINER OF THE GODS

KATIE MAXWELL

To Whom It May Concern: ~~If you find this letter, it means that I, January James, have fallen down the burial shaft of the Tomb of Tekhen and Tekhnet where I'm spending a month working as a conservator, and am probably lying at the bottom, dead from a broken leg and thirst. . . .~~

To whoever finds my sand-scoured, withered corpse: ~~I'm dead. It's the mummy's curse. Don't blame Seth, he was just trying to help, even if everyone does say he's the reincarnation of an evil Egyptian god. He's not. I know, because no one who kisses like he does can be truly evil.~~

Help! I'm stuck in Egypt with a pushy girl named Chloe, a cursed bracelet, and a hottie who makes my toes curl. . . .

CHLOE,
QUEEN OF DENIAL
NAOMI NASH

If you're reading this note, you're probably in the middle of the desert pulling it from the vulture-plucked bones of someone who used to be named Chloe Bryce.

Or maybe you're my poor, grieving parents who sent me to die in Egypt. A month at the Tomb of Tekhen and Tekhnet will look really good on your college resume, you said. Satisfied now, guys? Maybe you two didn't know I'd end up facing risks that would make Indiana Jones think twice—baths only every ten days, blistering heat, ancient tombs, mummies, a cursed bracelet . . . Of course, I did manage to kiss the dig's one hot guy—so you can console yourselves that I died somewhat happy!

Dorchester Publishing Co., Inc.
P.O. Box 6640
Wayne, PA 19087-8640

5377-2
$5.99 US/$7.99 CAN

THE REAL DEAL

Unscripted

Amy Kaye

Thanks to the reality-TV show that records her junior year in excruciating detail, Claire Marangello gets her big break: her own version of the TV show and a starring role in a Broadway musical. Plus Jeb, a way-hot co-star who seems to like her *that* way, and a half sister she didn't know she had. It's everything she's ever dreamed of.

Or is it a total nightmare? Her sister seems to be drifting away. Claire's not sure she can trust Jeb and his weird celebrity-centered world. The director seems to hate her; the dance steps are harder than she'd ever imagined. Claire's about to learn that while being a Broadway star is a challenge, real life has twists and turns harder than any onstage choreography and is totally . . . *UNSCRIPTED*.

Didn't want this book to end?

There's more waiting at **www.smoochya.com**:

Win FREE books and makeup!
Read excerpts from other books!
Chat with the authors!
Horoscopes!
Quizzes!